Maybe

A BALLAD OF MAYBES BOOK 1

MARK HAYES

Salthomle Publishing

Saltholme publishing
11 Saltholme Close
High Clarence
TS21TL

Book Layout © 2020 Saltholme publications

Maybe:
Mark Hayes -- 1st ed.
ISBN 9798615166709

Maybe

Contents

Chapter one

A Damp and Bloody Funeral

"A funeral amidst a drizzle, is there anything more depressing?" Benjamin West asked the universe in general.

"A thunderstorm?" replied his companion, on behalf of the universe, without any touch of sarcasm in his voice, though Benjamin had his suspicions.

"Ever literal, Gothe," Benjamin remarked under his breath, sighing, and not for the first time that day. In truth, however, his bleak mood was less to do with his companion's irritating mannerisms and more to do with the way his day was turning out. He had not expected to be standing in the greasy London rain, listening to a clearly bored priest going through the motions as he lay to rest another poor victim of smog-bound Cheapside. Quite aside from any other concerns, he did not feel correctly attired for the occasion. His royal blue tailcoat and red silk shirt stood out among the black-clad gathering of ill-fitting morning suits and dresses. It helped not at all that most were worn by those more used to the practical canvas and leathers of jobbing engineers, who looked just as out of place themselves, clad as they were in their Sunday best and burial clothes. Indeed, this just made him feel all the more incongruous in his own carefully tailored attire.

In fairness, he had not come to Cheapside intent on seeing a man laid to rest, or he would have dressed for such an occasion, but this knowledge did little to stop him feeling uncomfortably like a popinjay among the sparrows. It was distressing in all honesty, not that Benjamin had anything against the working classes. Indeed, it was one of their number he had made the journey down to Cheapside to call upon, or more correctly, to recruit for his cause. To be exact, he had come to see an old acquaintance of his father's. A man his pater had vouched safe to be the finest mechanical engineer in the Empire and considering the circumstances, a man Benjamin West was eager to meet. Sadly, however, that was no longer likely to happen, as the mechanic in question, who was known by the name Maybe, was the man who at this juncture had been boxed up and was being placed in the eight by three hole in the ground.

"Well, you asked, West, and it clearly would be worse to attend a funeral in a thunderstorm," Gothe half muttered back, having heard his master's utterance. There was an edge to his tone which from anyone else Benjamin would put down to irritation. This may have had much to do with the former manservant being slowly drenched alongside him. The hulking man's mutton-chop whiskers were already dripping and slicked flat to the sides of his face, which gave his already pale countenance a somewhat pallid appearance.

Benjamin exhaled frostily with not entirely sincere exasperation and a degree of resignation falling upon him as to how this conversation was likely to go. Gothe could be a difficult conversationalist at the best of times. Regardless of such reservations, he ventured an opinion anyway.

"Perhaps, but I cannot help but feel a thunderstorm would add a certain dramatic flair to the occasion, Gothe. Give it an air of the Shakespearian, some nuance of the theatrical, a bit of panache, if you will," Benjamin told his man.

"If you say so," Gothe replied with the tiniest hint of disapproval in his tone. Though it was hard to detect a difference between this and his tone at any other time.

"I do, Gothe, I do. A thunderstorm would give the occasion drama at least, and thus would be better than being buried in this depressingly relentless and uncommonly grey drizzle," Ben said as a drip of cold rain found its way down the back of his shirt.

"I'm not sure the deceased cares, either way, West," Gothe replied, which could have been considered a dry remark, had anything about the occasion been dry.

Benjamin gave the former manservant a weary look but bit off an irritable retort. Such would, he decided, be in poor taste given Gothe's unfortunate condition. Instead, he turned his gaze back to the funeral party and fell into a sombre silence as the priest droned on, the vicar's monotone voice giving Benjamin the distinct impression that the cleric was just going through the motions. Another by rote service for another soul lost in London's gloom. Too bored by the task to even speed things up to get out of the rain. *Or perhaps*, Benjamin considered, *he finds some disreputable joy in having a funeral party stay in the drizzle as long as possible*. Benjamin would not have ruled that out; the priest's dead grey eyes were the eyes of a bitter man.

The drizzle continued without relent, as did the priest. Until, after what seemed an interminable time, he slowly came to the end of the rites and allowed the coffin to be lowered slowly into the muddy ground.

As they were standing on the periphery of proceedings, Benjamin and Gothe found themselves waiting while a line of mourners took turns to pay respects to the woman in a widow's veil. The priest first, a gnarly hand held out for his due payment, taken with a nod of the barest respect on receiving his tithe, before he commenced stalking off up the graveyard towards the next funeral party a few graves along.

Then, as was the way of things, it was the turn of less holy but far worthier men. Most were stout and balding. Men of a certain age, and a certain type. Each with stubby calloused fingers which, though dutifully scrubbed with caustic soap, bore hints of oil and grease within the recesses of split and broken nails. Mr Maybe's peers all, and all in fairness turned out in their best to see a good man go into the ground.

Interspersed between those who worked with grease and gears were tradesmen and the odd woman or two that was not in tow as an engineer's wife. They had cleaner hands with less rough edges, hands used to handling money not metal, Benjamin did not doubt, but their respects were all paid the same way. A proffered hand, a look of condolence, a few words of expressed regret and then they moved off. Shambling back through the drizzle to their places of employment, the passing of a good man marked and now forgotten while the woman in the widow's veil waited in the rain for the last of them to pass.

Benjamin was half tempted to just turn and go. He and Gothe had only hung about on the fringes of the service out of respect. *Besides*, he considered, *it's not as if I actually knew the man*. Save, that was, through his father's journals, and if Gothe had then he had given no indication of it. Not that this was unusual for his former manservant who could teach a stone about being taciturn. *But really what words of comfort could I offer? Sorry your husband's dead, I came to offer him a job*. That did not strike West as much in the way of condolence.

However, wait he and his former manservant did all the same. Not out of a sense of duty in his case, but because he was profoundly aware of just how disapproving Gothe would be if they did indeed leave without paying their respects. Gothe had very firm opinions when it came to matters akin to funerals and the paying of respects to the deceased. Opinions which Benjamin did admit were understandable given the former manservant's condition, so it was mainly out of respect for Gothe that he waited in turn despite the drizzle. Respect and an ardent desire to avoid the sulking he would have been forced to bear had they done otherwise.

As the last of the other mourners shuffled off into the gloom, Benjamin walked up to take his turn, suddenly acutely aware once more that his attire was less than suitable. Gothe at least was in dressed black, but then Gothe had habitually dressed for funerals for a decade or more since he unexpectedly turned up at his own. This was why Benjamin kept his eyes averted groundward in order to avoid what he surmised would be the disapproving gaze of the widow.

"My sincere condolences, Madame. Your husband was a fine man," he said to the hem of a heavy black morning gown, without looking up.

Gothe coughed pointedly at his side, and Benjamin assumed this was to urge him to say more, so he feigned a cough himself to hide his embarrassment and continued. "Yes, a fine man, your husband, much respected by his peers and I would venture well thought of in the wider community."

Gothe coughed again, louder this time, and Benjamin felt a shape elbow jab into his side. *God's teeth*, he thought, *what more does the man expect me to say to the woman. It's not like I even knew the man.* Taking a deep breath, disgruntled, he tried once more. "Yes, much respected, I am sure we will all miss your husband greatly."

Gothe's cough developed a disapproving, "West," in between exaggerated throat clearing. This was enough to make Benjamin snap round his gaze angrily from the ground to his former manservant.

"Damn it all, Gothe, is there really a need for…?" he snapped before the pained expression on his companion's face brought him up short and he remembered where he was. That and the injection of an irritated feminine voice whose owner barely seemed to be holding back her own temper.

"What your friend is trying to inform you of, Sir," that voice said, with all the venom of a long tiring day behind those words, "is that it is highly unlikely you've ever met my husband. Indeed, that is an event some would say was impossible, unless of course, you mean my future husband, which would seem somewhat presumptuous of you as I've yet to meet any man whom I'd agree to marry, or indeed wished to."

"My apolo…" Benjamin found himself stuttering out. Only to have his words cut short as the tirade he was facing from the young woman in front of him was far from over.

"For your information, it is my father I'm burying here today. Who was indeed a fine man but one whom it seems obvious to me you have never met. Gods, from the look of you didn't come here for his funeral either, unless you lack the most basic grace of a child. You, Sir, are clearly dressed for carousing at Wandsworth docks not paying your respects, something you seem woefully incapable of doing to listen to you talk. So, tell me, who the hell are you and why the hell are you here?"

Benjamin suspected that behind her veil her eyes were blazing, and in truth he was not sure he blamed her. All the same, he felt more than a little aggrieved. His pride, of which he had too much according to some, was stung, not least by the dig about carousing on the docks. *Does she not recognise good tailoring when she sees it?* he thought. *I'm hardly wearing flashy glad rags. What does she take me for? Some dressed up ner-do-well?* He felt his ire rising at the very idea but forced himself to push it back down with the consolation that if she lived in Cheapside, it was perhaps of little surprise she did not recognise fine clothes when she saw them.

Beside him Gothe made a pointed grunt and nudged him once more. Doubtless his former manservant had observed his hackles rising.

Benjamin took a breath, collected himself, stopped looking down at the hem of her skirt and raising his eyes tried to explain. Not least because in fairness he had no wish to pile more misery on the young lady's shoulders today of all days.

"Allow me to express my regret… Miss Maybe?" he said with a note of inquiry, leaving a moment for a response which was not forthcoming. Perturbed by this lack of social graces, he coughed slightly to cover his embarrassment before continuing. "My name is Benjamin Edward West. I came down to Cheapside today with my…" He found himself at his usual loss when introducing Gothe to anyone and floundered slightly. "With Mr Gothe here," he recovered and continued, "in order to make your father's acquaintance. On finding his workshop shut up and a sign on the door saying 'Gone to a funeral', we made our way here as it is the closest grave… place of burial… hoping to find him here. It was not until we arrived that we discovered, to our misfortune, that the funeral in question was your father's, and as such had no time to change into more suitable attire. But as we were here, it seemed that the only correct and polite thing to do was to remain for the service and pay our respects, all things considered."

The veiled woman before him turned her head to the side slightly, took a long hard look at Gothe, then turned her gaze back to Benjamin.

"Why?" she said to him.

"I'm sorry?" he replied, the obliqueness of the question catching him off guard.

"So you have said. But that does not answer my question. Why?"

"I, erm… what sorry?"

"Why stay to pay your respects to a man you have never met?" she expanded, a note of exasperation in her voice.

"And for that matter, while you're at it, why did you wish to make his acquaintance in the first place? Tell me, y'lordship, do you always require every question explained, because I would imagine that makes conversation with you somewhat tiresome?"

The petulance of the third question grated on Benjamin's nerves to the extent that he was about to lose his temper when he heard footsteps on the flagstone path that ran off to the side of the graves and a new voice interrupted the conversation. Which, if truth be told, Benjamin welcomed, given how badly the conversation was going.

"Miss Maybe," the voice said, "my commiserations upon your loss. I hope perhaps I can… spare you some extended grief, by helping you to divest yourself of your father's holdings."

It was, Benjamin determined, a voice with all the charm of a disused spoil heap – dusty, gritty and promising nothing of value. He turned towards the speaker, feeling an odd sense of revulsion even before seeing him. One which did not lessen when he did. The speaker was a skeletal man of advanced years. Walking with the aid of a silver-handled cane shaped into some form of animal head, though Benjamin could not see exactly what kind of beast the vile individual chose as a totem.

The man stooped because his back was bent, or hunched heavily on one side, be that a defect of birth or an ailment of old age, Benjamin chose not to guess. Perhaps as an attempt to hide the deformity, the man affected a heavy opera cloak which hung off his shoulders, its red lining flapping in the breeze, which seemed frankly ridiculous in the circumstances, as did his ill perched top hat. If ever a man did not suit a topper it was this one. It didn't even serve a purpose as to protect him from the drizzle. An umbrella was being held over his head by one of two heavy-set men that flanked him. His companions were as large and as virile looking as he himself was wizened and frail.

Benjamin's first thought upon beholding the speaker fully was 'villain', indeed the man looked so much the penny dreadful villain at face value that Benjamin realised he must dismiss the idea. It seemed just too obvious to be true. The reaction of Miss Maybe, however, said differently.

"You're not wanted here, Harrington, you snivelling wretch. My father didn't sell out to you, and I'll damn his memory before I will!" she exclaimed, with such strength of feeling to her words that it made her earlier tirade against Benjamin seem frivolous in comparison.

The corpse-like figure in the top hat smiled, his grin showing yellowed, crooked teeth. "Miss Maybe, there is no need for this vitriol. I am sorry for your loss, truly I am. Your father was a fine man if a tad on the stubborn side. His demise, I assure you, was most unfortunate for us all," he said, placing stress on the 'unfortunate' with such saccharine sweetness, that it seemed at once bitter and full of spite. Benjamin considered this spoke much of the man's measure. That this was a man who enjoyed a little cruelty in his passions. There was an eagerness to his words, a connivance and no little threat. Something which became all the more obvious as the craven spoke on.

"It is sad we could not come to an understanding, your father and I. But fate can be a cruel mistress, can she not? But regardless of those past misunderstandings, I feel obliged to extend the same offer of coin I made your father to you now for his premises and stock. It is more than generous considering possible alternatives, as I told your father before his untimely demise."

"Untimely demise, you stinking pig born swine," the grieving woman behind Benjamin yelled, her words so full of spite and hate, it took him off guard.

"Calm yourself, Miss, Maybe," Benjamin heard himself saying, years of gentlemanly training coming to the fore. After all, what else could a gentleman do in such a situation? He moved to place himself between the three newcomers and the bereaved daughter, acting on instinct born of upbringing. It was obvious that the situation was turning ugly, and he was compelled to act. Behind him he heard Gothe grunt something similar and had no doubt the former manservant was moving to intercede also.

"I would listen to your friends, Miss Maybe," the man named Harrington said. "Let's not let this situation lead to violence. I do so despair of violence. All that is required is that you sell out to me and our business will be concluded without further unfortunate circumstances being required." One of his pet gorillas made a snorting sound, while the other just leered, adding their weight to his argument in the most obvious of ways. Not that either of them needed to. The thinly disguised threat behind his words was palpable enough.

What happened next, happened quicker than Benjamin could anticipate, let alone react to. From below the folds of her black morning dress Miss Maybe pulled forth a compact little derringer and with a primal howl of anguish raised it and let the tiny pistol cry out. The flash from the barrel stung his eyes and he ducked down long after doing so would have saved him from the bullet. Luckily for him he was neither the target of her wrath, or between her and it. But as he swung around to see who she had shot at he saw Gothe falling to the ground, a little bloody hole in the back of his heavy woollen coat.

"What the hell have you done?" Benjamin shouted as he made to catch his falling companion.

There was a cry of frustration mixed with anguish from Miss Maybe behind him, while the skeletal Harrington let out his own vitriolic cry. A cry that was something akin to triumph.

"Why, Miss Maybe, I do believe you have made a mess of things and done so before witnesses. Tut tut, now that was a mistake, I fear. I'm very much afraid I shall have to inform my good friends at Bow Street. Really, your family is having such a dreadful week. Still, what your father would not sell will now default to the crown and a few well-placed shillings will see it sold on to an interested party, I'm sure. As such, I shall bid you good day, my good woman. My condolences on your loss once more." The vile little man said it with such glee in his voice that Benjamin found his stomach turning with distaste.

With that the man and his well-trained gorillas beat a none too hasty retreat down the flagstone pathway. Neither Benjamin nor Miss Maybe bothered to watch them go. They were too busy with the mess before them.

"Oh God, I'm sorry, so sorry," Miss Maybe was saying. "He stepped across my aim. Why did he step across my aim?" The anguish in her voice was obvious, her previous anger drained away by the grief her actions had inflicted.

Benjamin's own anger was tempered as realisation of what had happened struck him. Whoever Harrington was, he had obviously been the target of Miss Maybe's ill-considered shot. All things considered, he realised, it was probably somewhat for the best that it struck Gothe.

"Is he... have I..." There was an edge of panic in the woman's voice. The combination of grief and adrenaline had given way to shock of some kind.

A great groan escaped from Gothe, as Benjamin pushed the fallen former manservant's arm over his shoulder and began the arduous process of helping him to his feet. "He'll li..." he started to say but cut the word off and corrected himself. "He'll survive. I dare say he's had worse, but we need to get him out of this rain and get the bullet out too. Your father's workshop's near. There will be tools there, won't there?"

Gothe grunted once more, presumably from the pain of the wound.

Even with the veil over her face Benjamin could tell Miss Maybe was confused. For a moment he just stood there with most of the weight of Gothe bearing down on him. His former manservant, unsteady on his feet, was leaning on him like a crutch, while she stood looking perplexed at this turn of events. He stumbled slightly and Gothe groaned once more, shifting against his shoulder.

"A little help here," Benjamin requested.

"What?" she asked, still shaken and a little bemused.

"Help me get him to the workshop," he said.

She continued to stare while he struggled, and for a moment Benjamin thought she might even refuse. Then in a snap she seemed to make up her mind about something. Her demeanour changed to one of solid determination, and she stepped forward, hooked Gothe's other arm over her shoulder, and prepared to lead them off.

"Are you sure we should be moving him," she asked as they started to carry the former manservant out of the graveyard through the drizzle.

"I'm wet enough already," he replied ardently. "I've no wish to get further soaked pulling a brass bullet out of his shoulder. It's a tricky job at the best of times."

She gave him what may have been a curious look, though as she was still wearing a veil it was hard to tell.

"You're a doctor?" she asked.

Benjamin managed a laugh. "No, Miss Maybe. Far from it."

"Then we should take him to one. It is hardly wise to go removing bullets yourself."

Benjamin paused for a moment, mostly to readjust his shoulder under Gothe's arm, and catch a little of his breath back. The former manservant was no light burden to be carrying even with help, though Gothe was taking some of his own weight, on unsteady legs. That was a blessing in Benjamin's opinion, as he was unsure they would have been able to move him otherwise. As they rested for those fleeting moments, he looked over at Miss Maybe and made a vain attempt to offer up an explanation.

"Gothe... Well, he wouldn't thank me for taking him to a sawbones, not least because they might wonder what he's doing walking around in the first place. It all tends to get rather complicated from then on, so it will be better all-round if I pull the brass myself."

Miss Maybe stared back at him, clearly confused. With her free hand she pushed up her veil and for the first time he saw her face clearly. Her skin was a surprising olive brown shade that spoke more of the southern Mediterranean than the smog-bound streets of Cheapside. But it was the strange tattooed spirals that wrapped themselves around her left eye and cheek that first caught his attention and seemed most out of place. It was some form of tribal design, reminiscent, he thought, of the type South Sea islanders were reputed to sport. But it was her bright, slate blue eyes that held his attention most. They were alive with inquiry and, if he was any judge, barely held back anger.

"Look, I just shot this man. Accidently or not, I'll not have him die because I didn't take him to a doctor. Do you really think I'm going to let you pull the bullet out in my workshop rather than get him proper care? Besides I'm in enough trouble as it is without having him die on my property." She said it with that same venom creeping into her tone he had witnessed before.

"He isn't going to die. We just need to get the bullet out before the wound heals up, is all. Believe me, Miss Maybe, there is no chance of him dying." He kept his tone as even as he could.

"If you're not a doctor, then how the hell could you know that?" she snapped.

Benjamin sighed heavily. Frankly, he was past any abiding wish to continue this conversation in the relentless drizzle. Besides, he decided, even if she was unlikely to believe what he said next, it might get her to drop her questions for a moment or two.

"Miss Maybe, I assure you, he isn't going to die," he told her. "I'm absolutely sure on that score, because he's been dead nigh on fifteen years. Now, if you please, can we get him to your father's workshop and out of this damnable rain?"

Chapter two

Doctoring a Dead man

Maybe's workshop was surprisingly claustrophobic for its size. A large building down by the Thames with its own private wharf that led out onto the river itself, it was a relic of the days when river barges rather than steam wagons were the main arteries of commerce in the capital. Within, it seemed every conceivable space was in use. Racking hung from the rafters to store long bars of metal or timbers. More racks lined the walls, storing everything from the largest barrels to the smallest tubs and strange bottles of oddly viscous fluids. There were boxes of machined parts, bolts and every considerable nut and pinion. Toolboxes and yet more racking held all the tools of an engineer's trade. A small steam engine lay dormant in one corner, partly covered by an oil-stained tarpaulin. From this, a heavy makeshift flue ran up beyond the rafters. Heavy gearing and belts could direct power from the engine to the machine drill or the lathe or several other devices, the use of which Benjamin could only guess. While in the centre of the overcrowded main room sat a heavy workbench made from railway sleepers on trestles. It was upon this ponderous contraption they laid out the groaning Gothe.

"I'll need a sharp knife, a needle and some coarse thread," Benjamin instructed, rolling Gothe onto his front to get a better view of the wound. Then added, in a hopeful tone. "Oh, and if you have it some alcohol. Gin for preference."

"Are you sure about this?" Miss Maybe asked, a note of concern in her voice, which was headily mixed with barely restrained panic.

Benjamin could not blame her. Chance was she was afraid she might yet prove to have 'killed' his former manservant. At the very least, this whole event would doubtless prove troublesome for her. Shooting people was generally an activity much frowned upon, even in a place like Cheapside.

"He's sure, Miss," Gothe said, his voice as monotone as ever but lacking the underlying strength it normally held. These were the first actual words he had spoken since being shot, words which brightened Miss Maybe's demeanour no end. Benjamin had no doubt she took them as a good sign. Indeed, Benjamin suspected this implied Gothe was starting to recover, but at the same time also implied a need for urgency. If the wound sealed itself, then removing the bullet would become very problematic and it had to come out, of that he was almost entirely sure.

"I'm so sorry… I wasn't aiming at…" Miss Maybe started saying.

"I know, miss. Don't worry yourself on my account," Gothe told her. "These things happen…"

She stiffened slightly and seemed almost offended by the offhand nature with which Gothe was treating events.

"That's quite beside the point…" she snapped back, and Benjamin found himself sighing loudly. It was all getting a little out of hand. In the short time he had known her, he had arrived at the conclusion Miss Maybe could make an argument out of the nodded greeting of someone as they passed by her on the street. He was beginning to find her a tad wearing, even while trying to make allowances for her recent bereavement.

"Now is not the time." Benjamin told her firmly, while attempting to pull a sleeve of Gothe's heavy coat clear of one arm.

Miss Maybe glared at him, and for a moment looked trapped between her need to apologise to Gothe and a desire to berate him.

"Knife, needle, thread, alcohol," he reminded her, pointedly.

He could tell she bit back some retort or other, but then she shook herself visibly and forced calm to her tone said, "Yes, of course." And went in search of the items he had listed. Though it was clear she was still far from full of the joys of spring.

Gothe groaned as Benjamin hauled the greatcoat over his back, then slid it off his other arm, and pulled it free of the former manservant. "Have a care will you," the patient said as the strangely glass-like resin that was, for want of a better word, his dried blood, made cracking snapping sounds as the coat was pulled away from his back.

"I'm doing my best here, Gothe, these are hardly ideal circumstances," Benjamin retorted irritably. Dealing with Miss Maybe's caustic mood was trying enough without Gothe's complaints thrown in the mix.

"Next time I get shot I will do so at a more convenient time, West," the former manservant replied with no hint of humour.

"You should. Damn fool. Why did you cross her sights to begin with? You must have seen she was about to shoot." Benjamin bemoaned while looking vainly for somewhere to hang Gothe's coat, before deciding that was a fool's errand and dumping it on a half empty shelf among boxes of odd-looking valves and machine parts which meant nothing to him.

"Did you?" Gothe muttered in reply.

"That's hardly the point. Woman's clearly a tad deranged with grief. How was I to know she had a weapon about her person, let alone that she would start taking pot shots at a funeral. I mean, who takes a pistol to a funeral, I ask you?"

Gothe craned his neck to look up at Benjamin from where he lay on the improvised workbench, serving as an even more improvised operating table, giving him a hard stare, then said "She's certainly a bit of a loose cannon, I'll grant you that. Not unlike someone else I could mention."

"What's that supposed to mean?" Benjamin snapped back, his temper flaring.

Gothe smiled at him thinly. "Nothing, West, nothing at all."

Benjamin glared back at the prone man, but any reply he might utter was cut short by the return of Miss Maybe, a bottle of gin in one hand, a knife and a small sewing bag in the other. She looked mildly flustered, her veiled hat thrown aside somewhere in the recesses of the workshop. Her dark hair now loose was a tangled mess of curls that hung past her shoulders.

"I hope these will do," she said, carefully placing the knife and everything else on the bench. She then set about rescuing a bottle of white spirit from a pocket in the recesses of her clothes. "We should be able to sterilise them with this," she added with a measure of composure before taking the bottle of London Dry, popping the cap and offering it to Gothe.

"It's not for me, miss," the former manservant replied with monotone courtesy.

She looked down at the man, perplexed for a moment. "But I assumed…"

"Not touched a drop in fifteen years. I can manage without now. Damn stuff was the death of me, swore I'd never touch it again." Gothe expanded, and gave her a weak smile, which looked forced and not a little strange; his was not a face made for smiling. "The gin's for Mr West, to steady his nerve."

"You can't be serious," she replied.

But Benjamin reached over and took the bottle from her hand, causing her to stare at him with a certain measure of disbelief as he took a long swig of the ruin of mothers.

"Perfectly," he said, when he paused between gulps. "Can't stand doing this sort of thing, so better to numb my senses a little first."

He took another swig before taking up the knife and hooking the blade under the former manservant's shirt. Then after he carefully pulled the blade up, slicing the linin in two, he retrieved the bottle and took a third swig, before pausing a moment and looking regretfully at the bottle in his hand, caught for a moment in two minds. Then he took final swallow before placing the bottle down a quarter empty.

"Are you trying to get drunk before you cut him open?" Miss Maybe said in a disbelieving tone.

"Better than him cutting me open sober, believe me," Gothe uttered unhappily from the table, then, taking a deep long breath, the wounded man closed his eyes and turned to face the wood of the workbench.

Benjamin risked a smile at Miss Maybe, though it was a grim smile at best. Then in defiance of the disbelieving expressing that crossed her feature, he took one last swig of the gin, and regretfully, poured the rest of the bottle over the wound in Gothe's back. The former manservant shuddered and let out a low groan of pain, but nothing more.

Painfully aware she was watching him Benjamin took up the bottle of white spirit and poured it over the knife, before taking out a matchbook from his trouser pocket, lighting a sprig and setting the blade to its flame.

She shook her head at him, and "harrumphed" loudly, before stalking off again behind some of the racking.

Damn, we need water, West realised as he watched the spirit burn off the blade, uncomfortably aware of how hot the blade's handle was getting. He was about to drop it when Miss Maybe reappeared, carrying a bucket of the needful. *Practical lass at least,* he thought to himself, and nodded his thanks, dousing the flaming blade which sizzled and sent up a cloud of steam.

Then, holding the blade out in front of himself with a degree of trepidation that Miss Maybe surely could not help but notice, 'unfortunately', he took a deep breath of his own and tried to gird his loins, as it were.

"You may not want to watch this bit," he said, trying to sound impassive. From the look she gave him he suspected she took his words as a challenge of sorts. The truth was he was talking as much to himself as to her and was struggling to keep his voice even.

"I watched as the bullet went in by my hand, I'll damn well watch it pulled free," Miss Maybe replied, surprising him with the iron in her voice.

Benjamin nodded towards her once more and took another fortifying breath. Then taking a last regretful look at the empty bottle of London's finest ruin, he got to his task. Taking the cleaned blade, he cut across the hole in Gothe's back, wincing as a dark red fluid, so dark to be almost black, that had to be blood seeped out. Though it seemed too viscous to be blood. It was too dark, too thick. Where it should have flowed it moved with the sluggishness of the Serpentine.

"That can't be right," Miss Maybe said, sounding confused.

"It's as right as it gets, Miss," Benjamin replied, setting the blade aside he pushed two fingers from each hand into the cut. Doing so made an odd glopping sound, like wellingtons in mud. Once he had his fingers inside, he tried to pull the flesh apart a little, while feeling around with his fingertips. Miss Maybe peered in over him trying to get a closer look. He was not sure if that was through morbid fascination or the desire to help.

"Damn," Benjamin exclaimed after a few minutes of this. "I just can't feel the bullet. I need something to hold the sides apart so I can get in properly, god knows what, forceps of some kind would be ideal." Fingers still in the incision, he started looking around for inspiration among the racks of tools before looking up at the nearest thing he had to a nurse in attendance. For a moment she just stared back at him and for the second time, ridiculously bad timing though it was, he noticed she had the most alluring blue eyes, which were currently staring intently into his. Eyes that seemed full of inquiry and intelligence.

"A moment," she said, breaking his distraction. Then turned and disappeared into the aisles of racking, leaving him fingers deep in the wounded back of his former manservant. She reappeared a few moments later bearing a pair of exceedingly long-nosed engineer's pliers.

"Will these do?" she asked.

"No, I need callipers or something. I need to hold the wound apart so I can get my hands in."

She huffed once more then shook her head at him. "For pity's sake. Just hold the sides apart." Saying this she walked around the worktable so she could get at the wound alongside him.

"You can't be serious, girl," Benjamin snapped at her.

"I put the damn thing in there I can damn well take it out," she snapped back with a mix of determination and no little frustration in her voice.

After a moment of passing disbelief, he nodded acquiescence, and pulled the wound apart once more.

"First things first," she said and poured white spirit over the nose of the pliers. "Matches?" she inquired.

Benjamin coughed, mildly embarrassed for a moment, and then explained he had put the matchbook back in his trouser pockets. He was about to take his hands out of Gothe to get them for her when she shook her head at him.

"Don't be ridiculous," she said and leant right over Gothe and stretched to fish the matchbook out of his pocket.

Benjamin was about to protest, as having a young lady rooting around in his trouser pockets was a long way past appropriate, but common sense and Gothe telling them to, "Get on with it," from amidst the operating table, overruled his sense of propriety. Though he had to bite his tongue slightly when she was rather rough about the whole thing as she fiddled around between loose change and the other detritus he was carrying about his person.

He was a little red-faced when she finally pulled the matchbook from The Forbes Gentleman's Club free, but if she noticed the embossed name on the matchbook, she did not react to the name. She just ripped a sprig free and struck it to burn off the white spirit in a vain attempt to sterilise the pliers.

After she dosed the pliers and motioned him to pull the two sides of the incision further apart, it was Benjamin's turn to watch with, he allowed, some little admiration and a degree of morbid fascination as she set about the task. She leaned fully over the wound to investigate the hole that was revealed, while holding the pliers tentatively, a worried crease on her forehead.

"I can't see the bullet," she said shaking her head. "I can't see anything. There's too much... too much... blood, if that's what it is."

"I don't wish to hurry you, Miss Maybe, but really this isn't really something we can take our time over," Benjamin told her with as much calm as he could muster.

"Do you want to do this?" she snapped back at him, meeting his eyes with a determined stare.

"Patently not," he replied honestly.

She continued to probe at the edges with the pliers while trying to get a better view. He could tell from the expressions she was pulling that she was far from revelling in the task. Gothe's blood had a sweet rotten smell to it, that could only be described as unpleasant. The flesh itself had a pallid colour to it which Benjamin knew did not look right to anyone. He didn't find it pleasant to look at either, if truth be told. It looked like, what it ultimately was, the flesh of a corpse. All be it a corpse that took regular baths and was reasonably good at personal hygiene. Which was a blessing in Benjamin's opinion.

"Damn it," she exclaimed angrily, though he suspected this time the anger was directed towards herself rather than anyone else. She banged the pliers down on the worktop, gritted her teeth and pushed her whole hand directly into the wound between his fingers, forcing it down into the viscera, grimacing as she did so. If the look on her face was anything to go by, she was clearly feeling as repulsed by the whole exercise as he was, but she but between the grimaces there was a look of pure determination on her face. Benjamin felt his stomach churn and found himself wishing heartily there was some more gin at hand.

After a minute or so of rooting around inside the incision, Benjamin saw a glimmer of triumph in her eyes. "I can feel something, right at the tip of my finger," she told him, then strained to push her hand in further. "Almost… got… it…"

"Careful, we don't want to tear the wound," he suggested.

Their eyes met and for a second he saw a flash of anger in hers, then she looked back to her task. "Just pull the sides apart a little more and I will have it," she as much as ordered him through gritted teeth.

Gothe groaned loudly but offered no other complaint as Benjamin doing as he was bid, pulled the wound still further apart, his fingers straining against the flesh. He watched as Miss Maybe pushed her hand in as far as she could, He could see she was trying to reach the bullet, searching with her fingertips through whatever viscera lay within the incision.

"Almost... all... most..." she said though he suspected she was talking as much to herself as to him, "All...Most..." her hand now so deep into the incision she was up to her wrist inside Goths back. Then elation flashed across her face, "Got it!" she announced triumphantly.

As she said this, the two of them up to their arms in gore, Benjamin heard a crashing bang and the sound of wood splintering and the door to the workshop exploded inwards and several men in police uniforms burst in...

Chapter three

Caught Red-handed

"We in the Metropolitan Police have a saying you know, 'Caught Red-Handed,' and I must say, I've found it's seldom so literally applicable, Miss Maybe," Inspector Grace of Bow Street stated in a bland toneless manner, which was a tone he had learned to adopt from his fellow officers back when he was serving in India whenever he was not entirely sure of what was going on, which he was not.

He knew, deep down to his core that a crime had been committed. He also knew that he had entered a Cheapside workshop at the side of the Thames to find the very woman he had been sent to arrest, a woman who stood accused of shooting a man, with her hand actually inside said individual, while her victim was lying face down on a workbench doing a very convincing impression of a corpse. A corpse smothered in thick dark fluid, which undoubtedly was blood, he was almost sure of that. Blood that was running out of an open wound, and all over the workbench.

Well not running exactly, running is not the word, seeping, that would be a better word, blood seeping all over the place, he considered, then added to that thought by thinking *blood really shouldn't seep like that… Or be more black that red. Blood definitely shouldn't be black and seeping…*

Two people stood over the victim. One of them clearly could only be Miss Maybe from the description he had been given. Standing there with her hands smothered in… Well, he told himself, *It's definitely blood,* for all it seemed to have treacle-like qualities. While the other person present was a man, who was equally caked in thick dark red, almost black, blood. A man who happened to smell like the inside of a gin palace and was aiding Miss Maybe in whatever foul act they were undertaking. It was as open and shut a case as it was possible to imagine.

'Caught Red-Handed' indeed…

Despite this, the reason he was not feeling entirely sure of himself, however, was the reaction he and his men had elicited when they came bursting into the workshop. To wit being told, in a loud and forceful voice, "Just shut up and wait over there."

As reactions to the police bursting in and catching a pair of criminals 'red-handed', it was original, he had to admit. And a reaction all the more perplexing as it came not from the criminals themselves. Instead the speaker of those particular words was, in defiance of all logic, appeared to have been the victim.

Faced with what seemed to be an impossible conundrum, the inspector decided to do what any good copper does when faced with a mystery that scuppers an otherwise clear-cut case, he tried to ignore it.

Instead, he resorted to the tried and tested method of getting on top of a situation by making a determined effort to sound confident and in charge. And so, he loudly repeated himself, with the strongly held belief, based on little more than wild optimism of a man with a half dozen constables behind him, that if he did so clearly and asserted his obvious authority, things would start to make sense. "I said, we have you caught red-handed, Miss Maybe!"

"We're a bit busy here, inspector," the lady in question replied, unperturbed and sounding more than a little irritable. Then she pulled her hand out of the victim's back and dropped something small and metallic onto the bench, where it bounced a couple of times before rolling onto the floor.

The inspector raised his police issue revolver, a rare item which he seldom brought out of his office drawer. But, as he told himself, when you were going to arrest a suspected murderess it's wise to do so armed.

"Miss Maybe, I really must insist you and your accomplice step away from the victim," he said evenly, trying to get a grasp on the situation.

The woman's accomplice shook his head with what seemed like disbelief and looked on the verge of protesting. However, Miss Maybe put her bloody hands down on the workbench, turned her head and met Grace's eyes evenly. She huffed at him sounding exasperated, then turned fully and began wiping her hands on the plain black dress she was wearing. It struck Grace that it was reminiscent of a widow's dress, doubtless chosen out of some misplaced sense of the dramatic, he concluded. If she had not being wearing black, he realised, her skirts would be a scarlet study of gore. Indeed, he ventured to himself, Mrs Tussaud would doubtless be delighted to learn the details of such a visceral image and might want to mount a display in her wax museum. Unseemly as such base exhibits clearly may be the museum had made a small fortune out of the bloody waxworks of old Jack's victims. There was, he knew, a certain renown to be had from being the arresting officer in such a case. Of course, he would deny taking any pleasure from this idea, no matter how much someone pressed him on the matter, it was unseemly after all. But still…

Grace found himself considering the look of rage in Miss Maybe's face. It was a mask of anger and frustration, no doubt at being caught in the act, the visage of a mad woman haunted by her victims. Perhaps they would find more bodies hidden in the recesses of this workshop. *I should summon The Times*, he thought to himself. *This could mean promotion, perhaps even memoirs. This could be the making of my career. Inspector Grace, the man who caught the bloody-handed murderess of Cheapside. It has a good ring to it.*

Grace brought himself up to his full height and puffed out his chest some more, raised his revolver and started to say in a firm tone, "Miss Maybe..."

"Oh, do shut up... Look the kettle's over there," she said, sounding irritated and pointing to the small kitchenette section of the workshop, a look that could have been described as disbelief on her face. "Have one of your constables make us all a nice cup of tea, will you, and we can get this mess sorted out once we're done here. We're probably out of milk but if someone nips to Mr Cohen's down the street, I'm sure he will be happy to lend you some."

"Tea?" the inspector said disbelievingly. "Tea? I don't think you realise how much trouble you're in, Miss Maybe."

"Actually, Sir, a cuppa sounds like a good idea," Constable Riley piped up behind him, a copper who the Inspector had noted on more than one occasion previously could always be relied upon to consider a tea break to be a good idea.

"I don't believe I'm hearing this. Tea? We've caught a murderess red-handed here, Constable Riley, and you want to stop for tea?"

"Well, she did offer, inspector, and it's not like she's going anywhere," Riley put in hopefully.

"God's teeth, man, will you get yourself over there and slap the cuffs on her," he said, waving his pistol like a conductor's baton in the direction of the macabre scene. Only to suffer a further interruption, this time from an unexpected source.

"If you're making tea, I wouldn't say no to a cup, milk and two lumps if there is sugar," said the source in question, which happened to be the bloody corpse of the victim that was laying on the workbench.

Frustration, caused by the way things seemed to be getting beyond his control, bubbled over within the

Inspector. Something his Constables were not entirely unused to. They could tell he was about to lose it a little, by the way his moustache had started quivering.

"We are not here to make tea. We are here to arrest a murderess, one indeed we have just caught in the very act of murder. We are the Metropolitan Police, as sanctioned by the Home bloody Secretary himself. We don't stop for tea when a murder is being undertaken before our very eyes. We act. God help us, what would the victim say if we were to pay such little regard to his murder as to stop for a cup of tea. I ask you?" the inspector shouted with a due amount of wrathful anger in his opinion.

"Erm, I think he said he'd like milk and two lumps, Sir," said Constable Riley, helpfully.

The fight went out of Inspector Grace. *When*, he considered, *a murder victim is going around asking for a cup of tea, someone has made a mistake.* He had the sudden and quiet horrible suspicion that someone might be him. He also suspected grimly that blustering it out seemed unlikely to be a successful strategy at this point in proceedings. He knew one thing for sure, however, that was that things like this ought not be allowed.

The young woman with the bloody red hands was no longer paying him the slightest bit of attention either, he noticed. She had instead turned back to whatever foul deed she was partaking in and asked her accomplice to pass her the needle and thread. Not even the slightest of regard for his presence or his pistol, that seemed damn well indecent somehow. It wasn't the kind of respect he was certain the newly formed Metropolitan Police should command. Still, it was clear there was more going on here than he had been led to believe. It would need some sorting out, that was for sure.

Grace took a deep breath, pointedly lowered his revolver, placed it back in the holster, straightened his overcoat and gave a slightly embarrassed cough.

"Milk and one for me then, Constable, be about your business now," he said, putting a brave face on it. Then he started looking around for a spare chair to park himself on, before, as an afterthought, he asked the murderess somewhat hopefully… "I don't suppose you have any rich tea biscuits at all?"

Chapter Four

The Untangling
of Events

Half an hour had passed by the time the man Inspector Grace was to learn was named Harrington crossed the broken threshold of the machine shop, with accompanying goons. By this point Grace had, somewhat apologetically, sent a junior constable to fetch a carpenter to repair the door. Meanwhile he, Constable Riley, Gothe and two other constables were sat on upturned buckets serving as stools, around a cable drum that had been laid on its side to serve as a table. Upon this sat a surprisingly clean china teapot, which Miss Maybe had dug out of a cupboard somewhere. In which a second pot of tea was mashing for all concerned.

Miss Maybe herself was busy washing her hands in the sink, trying to get the dark red gel-like substance that should have been blood from her hands and, more importantly, from under her fingernails with best coal soap. Mr West was taking his ease, leaning against the workbench awaiting his turn at the sink whenever Miss Maybe had finally finished her fastidious ablutions. His hands were still thick with blood. Luckily, the man had had the foresight to roll up his shirt sleeves. Unfortunately, the bloody stuff had still been splattered liberally on his garments and while Grace suspected he was pleased that he was not mourning the loss of his man Gothe, he was certainly mourning the loss of a good shirt.

"What the devil is going on here?" Harrington screeched on entering the workshop. His voice, like nails being dragged down a blackboard, cut through the peaceful air. "Why is this murderous woman not currently clapped in irons and in the process of being carted off. You, Sir, are you in charge here?" This last was directed at Grace, a fact made obvious by the way Harrington was waving his cane at him.

The inspector was ruffled by the tone of the new arrival, and less than happy with the way he was pointing the walking stick at him. As a rule, he did not take to people who pointed things at him, and having finally got a grip on his afternoon, he was in no mood to have it ruined once more by a pointer. Pointers were always trouble, he had found. Grace stood purposefully and brushed down his overcoat, his moustache bristling as his nose seemed to crinkle as if detecting a bad smell. Then in a tone of voice which balked no argument, he said, "I am indeed in charge, Inspector Grace of Bow Street, and as I'm in charge here, I will ask you, Sir, to mind your tone. There is a lady present."

Harrington was not it seemed a man who cared about those who balked no argument, sadly.

"Lady? I detect no lady, only the murderous harpy who shot a man not more than two hours ago in Cheapside cemetery. Why, Sir, I do my civic duty and send a runner to Bow Street, yet when I arrive here to see if justice has been done, I find you drinking tea while she washes the blood of her vile crime from her hands."

The outrage in the man's voice seemed forced. Grace had over the years met many a man who treated the law with contempt, save when they wished it used to their advantage. The newcomer, he suspected, was exactly that kind of man.

"I will not tell you to mind your tone again, Sir. If you do not temper it, I shall have you escorted from the premises. We intend to sort all this out once the young lady has had time to repair her appearance," Grace informed the skeletal Harrington, who he had an unreasonable urge to arrest for looking guilty in a built-up area. An offence which sadly was not on the statute book, but Grace was occasionally of the opinion it damn well should be.

"Washed the blood from her hands, you mean," Harrington broiled. Though with noticeably less venom. The man, Grace noted, seemed to have quickly concluded that things were not going to go quite the way he had expected. He was now simmering with resentment, while his two minders lurked behind him with all the intent they could muster under the circumstances.

"You're not welcome here," Miss Maybe stated in a subdued tone, though it was spoken with enough forthright indignation that Grace suspected it nevertheless held of undercurrents of anger and prospective violence.

Inspector Grace did not consider himself a man slow to realise when the mood of a room had changed, though this vanity was not always earned. He could, however, tell that whoever this man was, he and his goons had brought a nasty edge to the room and Miss Maybe's temperament had moved toward the suspect. He noted also that her erstwhile compatriot, the man whom she had introduced as a Mr West, had noticeably stiffened and was eyeing the newcomers with a considered stare of contempt.

There were, it was safe to say, things afoot here. Things to which he was not entirely privy. As the man in charge, it therefore behoved him to get a grip on the situation. Which was, he considered, a shame because he was just looking forward to a second cup of tea.

"Let me handle this please, Miss Maybe," Grace stated with all the authority he could muster. "I am after all the officer of the law here."

"Well, as that is the case, I demand you arrest her," Harrington insisted, pointing his cane once more, this time at the young lady in question. Grace noted the chilly look the blaggard drew from the young lady by doing so.

"And who, Sir, are you to make such a demand? Your name, Sir, and your business here?" the inspector snapped, matching the intruder's tone.

Harrington looked at the inspector with a frosty expression. For a moment, that look made the inspector wonder if he had made another mistake. There were some gentlemen in London you were wise to recognise, after all. Particularly if you were a member of the constabulary. Judges and Ministers of the Crown, for example, were known to take a dim view of policemen attempting to arrest them. It was not a wise career move, unless the move you desired was decidedly backwards and Inspector Grace was a man who always sought to take great care of his career. He had joined the force after returning from India, having spent five years serving as an officer with the Punjab rifles. The mutiny put pay to his ambitions as a man of the Raj and earned him a game leg. The smog-filled streets of London were however far safer than life in Bengal and he had traded on a reputation as a minor war hero to gain his position in Sir Robert Peel's finest. He had determined from the start that he wished to rise as high as possible within the ranks of the new force. As such, he had decided quite early that there was wisdom to be had in treating those of wealth and privilege with kid gloves. In particular, those who on occasion had one trouser leg shorter than the other. With these thoughts in mind he almost retracted his question in light of the man's icy stare. But the inspector was having a bad afternoon and irritation got the better of his sense of self-preservation.

"I asked you your name, Sir, I shall have it or I shall have the constables here escort you to Bow Street where you can give it to the desk sergeant," Grace demanded a second time.

"I, Sir, am James Harrington the Third, and I demand this woman be arrested. I and my companions, Misters

Instrument and Blunt here, bore witness to her shooting a man in the back not two hours ago. As any good subjects of Her Majesty would, we sent word of this heinous act to Bow Street. Then we made our way here at our first convenience to make sure she was indeed rightfully arrested. I demand therefore you undertake to do your duty, Sir, and arrest her forthwith. Demand it, I say."

"That's a lot of demanding, Mr Harrington," injected Mr West in a laconic tone from where he leant against some wall racking.

Harrington rounded upon West and started pointing at him with his cane.

He's damn fond of that cane, Grace thought to himself, adding bitterly. *Bloody pointers, you can never trust the bloody pointers.* He grimaced as Harrington started shouting the odds once more.

"You, Sir, you witnessed the villainous act yourself. Blast it, man, it was your own companion she shot. I am surprised you are not joining your voice to mine own in insisting upon her arrest," the aforementioned pointer inferred.

"I did indeed, and I assure you Miss Maybe had no intention of shooting Gothe. It was clearly nothing more than an unfortunate accident," Mr West replied calmly, repeating what he had already vouched safe to Grace earlier.

"No intention… No intention… Oh I'm sure of that, Mister…?" Harrington said, and left that 'Mister' hanging, leaving the inspector in no doubt that the two men had never been formally introduced. Mr West however remained silent, a laconic bent to the thin smile on his lips. He, Grace noted, was obviously wise enough not to volunteer such information to the odious Harrington, who only became slightly more flustered as the pause drew out. Then he coughed to cover his embarrassment and continued with his own diatribe, "I'm sure she had no intention of shooting your Mr Gothe, because I've no doubt she had every intention of shooting me."

This was new information to Inspector Grace. That the shooting of Mr Gothe had been no more than an unhappy accident had been well established over a refreshing cup of tea. He had not been aware the reason for that accident had been because there was another intended target. This nugget shed a new light on the matters to be certain. Though having spent only a few minutes in the company of James Harrington the Third he found had a degree of sympathy with anyone wishing to shoot the man. He could have quite cheerfully done so himself there and then. Be that as it may however, shooting at people in general was not something to be encouraged, Grace believed, and so he turned his gaze back to Miss Maybe, a note of inquiry within it.

Miss Maybe simply shrugged while drying her hands on a towel, having finally removed the last of the blood from them. The inspector, however, held her gaze and did so long enough that she became inclined to speak. When she did, it was in a calm measured tone. A tone which Grace had come across before in India. A tone which held within it a suggestion of the simmering rage beneath it.

"What cause could I possibly have to shoot you, Mr Harrington?" she said, but Grace could hear the challenge in her words.

"What cause, why what cause does a perfidious woman of ill intent need to shoot a man who merely wished to express his sorrow at the passing of her father. A man who sought only to offer some little condolence to that effect," Harrington replied coldly. Which gave the inspector no doubt there was much more to all this than he knew.

"What cause indeed?" Mr West said laconically, leading Grace to suspect whatever cause there may have been, Mr West, who was an undoubtedly a gentleman from his appearance, if you made allowances for the blood stains on his shirt, saw nothing untoward in Miss Maybe's actions.

"Have you proof of this?" Grace asked, though he could make a fair guess at what answer was likely to come his way.

"My men here witnessed the act," Harrington said firmly.

As if that constitutes proof of any kind, Grace thought, though he knew it may well have done so to a magistrate if it was undisputed, particularly considering the woman was, well, 'colonial,' even if these men were clearly in Harrington's employ at the time.

"As did I, Inspector," Mr West said, "and I can assure you I did not see Miss Maybe shoot at this man," He added then stepped towards Grace while fishing in his pocket, from whence he pulled his card, which he offered to the inspector.

Grace looked at the small square of card with some distaste then took it. He was mildly put off by the fact the man's hands were still covered in blackish… for want of another word, blood. He had no doubt the offer of the card was a deliberate ploy by Mr West to establish his credentials. Regardless a courteous glance at the heavily smudged card was required by the form of such things. West seemed to be a gentleman of some standing, while James Harrington the Third was undoubtably a short step up from a common street thug. *The Third is right, he is very much a third…* Grace thought to himself. The word of *The Third* and of his men counted for little in comparison to that of a gentleman's.

Grace smiled beneath his moustache. Of course, he could not be seen to take sides in this sordid little affair, but he had already determined he had more sympathy with the lady in question than with 'The Third,' and Mr West had just placed her at the advantage. Something which Harrington, who backtracked somewhat, clearly realised as well.

"Be that as it may, the fact remains she shot a man. That's still a crime in England, I believe. As such, Inspector, I demand once more that you do your duty and arrest this harlot at once."

Grace bristled at this. "I have warned you to watch your tone, Sir, I shan't do so again."

Anger flared in the eyes of the skeletal little man. He snorted loudly and looked as if he may be about to launch into yet another diatribe. His two goons made to loom menacingly as their employer grew angrier. But then the moment passed, Harrington seemed to think better of it and a look of calm came over the man's face.

"My apologies, Inspector. I'm a man of passions when my blood runs hot. I'm sure, however, you can see your duty? That Miss Maybe shot a man is clearly apparent to you, as there is no denial from anyone to that effect. It strikes me therefore you need to arrest her, and place her before a justice of the peace, it is your duty. After all, it's not for you to determine guilt, I believe, Inspector, but to place the burden of that determination before the court," Harrington said with an oiliness that made Grace feel slightly unclean just listening to it.

Grace also found himself balking at the idea of Harrington as a man of passion, a more passionless individual he found hard to imagine. But he also knew that for all that sickly lawyer speak the man was correct in what he said. The inspector felt decidedly queasy as he realised he was going to have to do as the odious Harrington insisted, no matter his personal opinion on the matter. Somewhat resigned to this outcome, he turned back to the lady in question, intent on doing his duty…

There was a loud cough, doubtless intended as an interruption to proceedings. Grace looked for the source and realised it emanated from Mr Gothe, who commenced clambering to his feet. His ruined shirt discarded, the man wore only his heavy overcoat, which hung open before a chest covered in coarse black hair.

Harrington's face went paler than before, if that was possible. It was clear to Inspector Grace that up until this point the man had not actually realised one of the men sat at the table was actually the victim himself. It may also have had something to do with Gothe being taller and broader than both of Harrington's thugs. Mr West's former manservant, as West had introduced him earlier, was an imposing figure. All the more imposing as he had a way of looking past you as if you were not there half the time. Which given the way he was currently looking at Harrington would have made Grace feel some sympathy for him, if he had not already found himself determined to despise the man.

"Miss Maybe did not shoot a man," Gothe stated with oddly arid dryness to his voice, and then began fishing in the recesses of his overcoat. A few moments of searching produced a dirty brown folded piece of paper which looked like a relic of bygone times. He stepped over and handed it to the Inspector, who took it and opened it with care. Not least because it looked liable to fall apart in his hands.

Grace took a moment to read it carefully. Then took a long appraising look at Gothe, then West, then pulled his gaze back to Gothe, the words 'former manservant' crossing his consciousness. *Former manservant. Former manservant. Former.* It took a moment or two to fully sink in. He looked down at the crumpled piece of paper once more, then up at Harrington, and his thin smile grew into a grin. At times a policeman's job is somewhat thankless. Seldom are people pleased to see you. When they are, they are demanding you do this or that because it suited their purpose. More often than not you have to do as they say and up until reading the paper before him the inspector had been certain that he would have to arrest Miss Maybe in the end. Even if the case was later to be dismissed, the inspector was detective enough to know that Harrington wanted her arrested not out of some sense of civic duty but some nefarious reason of his own. Being able to put pay to whatever the repulsive little man was up to was going to brighten his day no end, he decided.

"I see, well that puts a different light upon it," the inspector said. "Former Manservant… very good…" he said and allowed himself a small chuckle. "Now then let's see, ah yes, Constable Riley?"

"Yes Sir?"

"You and Constable O'Toole escort this gentleman and his…" He struggled for the appropriate word. "…friends, from the premises before we have to arrest them for trespass as I am sure the proprietor, which I believe would be Miss Maybe over there, did not give them leave to enter." He glanced away from the fuming Harrington to the lady in question.

She smiled at him, which he found a remarkably rewarding experience. "I most certainly did not, Inspector."

He nodded in return. "I thought as much. Mr Harrington be so good as to be on your way," he said and preceded to usher him towards the door.

"What? How dare you, Sir?" Harrington said, now more than a little irate, and confused at the turn of events.

"Now now, Mr Harrington. Lets be off with you, and I will suggest you will do well to keep a distance from this establishment from now on. I would be most galled to hear of you harassing Miss Maybe's establishment in future," Grace said, before taking up his teacup and having a sip of what was now lukewarm tea.

Fuming, Harrington made his leave with Misters Instrument and Blunt being escorted to the door by the two constables. The inspector retook his seat and placed the teacup on one side while Mr West commenced cleaning himself up in the sink and Mr Gothe put a fresh pot on.

After a few minutes Constable Riley returned and positioned himself close to Inspector Grace, a look of confusion on his freckle spattered face.

"Sir, I'm not sure I understand," he said quietly after a moment.

Grace looked over at Gothe for confirmation and was unsurprised that Riley's attempted circumspection was overheard. The lad had a lot to learn in the inspector's opinion. Not least was to actually say things as quietly as he thought he was saying them.

Gothe nodded silently, clearly not overly bothered who was taken into confidence on the matter, so Grace handed Riley the piece of paper he had received from the looming former manservant a few minutes before.

The reading of the piece of paper took a while as Constable Riley may have had his letters, but it was more a case of holding them hostage than full ownership. But read it he did...

Professor Virixes
House Of Hebrew Prestidigitation
Bill of sale
1 flesh golem
Formerly Albert Gothe deceased
To Formerly Albert Gothe deceased
For the sum of 18d 6s
June 12th 1884

Riley looked up at the looming Mr Gothe with whom he had been sharing a pot of tea only a few minutes before. "Well blow me," the constable said. "The world just keeps getting stranger."

Chapter Five

Two Tales of One City

The inspector had finally vacated the workshop an hour later but not before stationing Constable Riley by the broken remains of the door. A carpenter had been sent for, but due to the late hour would not arrive until the following morning to repair the damage done by the hasty entrance of Her Majesty's constabulary.

Watching the inspector depart, Benjamin witnessed Miss Maybe exhale a momentary sigh of relief, but she had still looked nervous and a tad skittish to his eye. Not, all considered, that he blamed her much given the events of the day. Gothe was making himself busy brewing yet another fresh pot for them all and as for Benjamin himself, he was still mourning the loss of a good shirt. But otherwise he found himself slightly at a loss as to what to do next. His journey to Cheapside had, it seemed, been a waste of time and energy. The unfortunate circumstance of Mr Maybe's death put all his plans in issue. It was vexing to say the least, though he was not so self-absorbed as to not admit to himself that Maybe's death was probably more vexing for the engineer himself. Though that said, with the exception of Gothe, he suspected the dead cease to be vexed by anything, and he was not entirely sure he had ever seen Gothe vexed come to that.

To top off everything else, the gin Benjamin had guzzled so liberally to do the necessary and remove the offending bullet earlier, was now starting to enact its revenge in the form of a growing hangover. He felt an overwhelming desire to head it off with a liberal application of more mother's ruin. Yet instead of taking his leave, he remained in the workshop of the man who was so inconveniently deceased. He knew why of course, he was a man who prided himself on being aware of his shortcomings. Alongside a certain amount of vanity, and a taste for London Dry which occasionally got the better of him, he was also afflicted with a terrible case of curiousness, and much about Miss Maybe and her situation remained a curiosity unsatisfied.

So now he was watching her, trying to take her measure and determine a way to get a few answers. She had calmed down a great deal once the initial panic of removing the bullet had passed and despite himself, he could not help but be impressed at how she had taken charge of that situation. He admitted to himself that he had not been entirely in control of matters. He seldom was when things got a little hairy, that too was another of his shortcomings, he admitted to himself. A tendency towards panicked desperate measures with little forethought. She however had been utterly focused on the task at hand, refusing to be thrown from her course even when the police battered down the door. But even now with the inspector gone, there was still a hint of tension around her, an edge, an itch unscratched. Something to do with the odious Harrington, Benjamin suspected. And there lay another mystery. No matter how odious he may be, generally speaking it was an overreaction to try to shoot someone for that alone. After a few moments considering this, a thought struck him.

"He'll be back, won't he?" he said, speaking his thought out loud. Not through any real intent to vocalise it. Perhaps it was just a subconscious desire to break the silence. But he noted the tense reaction that crossed Miss Maybe's face when he did.

"I expect so," she said, and no more, nervously fidgeting with her dress. An odd expression crossed her face. It was clear she was trying to make a decision of some kind.

Benjamin was tempted to say more, but instead he let the silence between them drag out. He thought it better to give her a chance to open up a little than force the conversation.

A moment or so later she looked over towards him and let out a breath he had not realised she was holding, before looking him firmly in the eye.

"If you're referring to Harrington then yes, he'll be back."

"It was him you tried to shoot, wasn't it?" Benjamin said, knowing he was stating the obvious but not knowing how else to approach the subject. As she nodded admittance to that, he added, "Would it be impertinent of me to ask why?"

"Highly," she said with false snootiness. Then to his surprise she favoured him with a remarkably broad grin which brought her face to life in, he considered, a surprisingly delightful way, before continuing, "But I suspect I owe you an answer all the same. If not you, then your good friend Mr Gothe over there certainly. He did after all catch the bullet for me."

"That's one way to put it..." Benjamin agreed, wondering if she realised it was entirely possible Gothe had done just that in some respects. Having had time to get to grips with it all, Benjamin was not entirely sure that Gothe had not taken the bullet on purpose. It was convenient to say the least that the girl had not actually shot Harrington, no matter how odious the man was. A distraught young woman at a funeral shooting dead a man was after all something that could be problematic. He certainly would not put it past Gothe to intervene for reasons of his own. He was entirely determined to ask his former manservant if that was actually the case when he got him alone. Though he was almost certain he would not get a straight answer.

Miss Maybe, took a long breath, which he suspected was her stalling for time. Perhaps, he considered, she was trying to think of some convincing story she could spin him. But then he noticed the note of pain in her eyes that, if nothing else, convinced him she would be telling him the truth, or at least some of it.

"Do you know how my father died, Mr West?" she asked him and he realised that this was the missing piece of the jigsaw, obvious now he thought about it.

"You suspect Harrington had a hand in it?" he said. '*Not a death of natural causes, I should have known,*' he added to himself. It all made a horrible kind of sense with that question. He and Gothe had come down to Cheapside on the train, not knowing Mr Maybe was dead until they arrived to find the workshop closed up and a sign on its door directing people to the funeral. But exactly how he died was a question that had not even occurred to him. His assumption was it had been natural causes or causes as natural as they get in a place like Cheapside. Bad air, poor food, poorer housing, infection, disease. There were lots of 'natural' reasons people died in the slums. Indeed, he had not considered it polite to raise the subject. But if it had been something else, something that was decidedly not natural causes, that had done for Mr Maybe, well that complicated matters. His own enterprise had been dogged with bad luck since its inception. Bad luck he had begun to suspect was also far from just that, but deliberate obstacles being placed in his way to block his endeavours. *But surely this can't be connected*, he found himself thinking, somewhat more in hope than expectation. He had a sinking feeling his own business might be wrapped up in Mr Maybe's death. He was not sure he liked the connotations of that feeling. Even less so when he was looking into the eyes of the man's daughter… the girl before him with eyes filled with grief.

"No, Mr West, I don't suspect his involvement in my father's death. To suspect would allow for some doubt. I have no doubt. I'm utterly certain that James Harrington killed my father. Or caused him to be killed on his order, which much amounts to the same thing."

"Then surely, the police..." Benjamin began, but his words fell away due to the look she gave him. A look somewhere between amusement and pity.

"Oh... I know he had a hand in my father's death, Mr West, but I unfortunately have nothing you could call proof. This is Cheapside, Sir, and Harrington... he as good as runs the place. Cheapside is a shithole, I'll grant you that, but he is the king of this shithole. So, without proof... In fact, even if I had proof... no one would touch him. Half the damn runners around here are in his pocket and the other half want to be. Cheapside stinks of shit but none of it sticks to Harrington, none of it..." she told him, making no attempt to disguise the bitterness of her words, and Benjamin blanched slightly at the words she chose, unused to a woman being quite so colourful in her language.

"But Inspector Grace... he ran him off happily enough," he argued.

"The Inspector? He's from Bow Street and Harrington's pockets don't reach that far. But we don't see them down here over much, they let the local nick deal with the likes of them around here. Not sure why Harrington would send for coppers from Bow now I think about it? It's odd," she said, a puzzled look crossing her face.

There was a loud throat clearing cough of dramatic proportions and Benjamin, who recognised this 'subtle' approach to joining a conversation, looked over at Gothe who was walking towards them with a pot of tea in hand.

"To get you well out of the way, Miss, I would venture, probably because he wants something here and wanted it all watertight legal wise," the former manservant suggested.

Benjamin did not doubt the Gothe was correct. For all his usual stoicism he had a habit of cutting to the heart of things. Miss Maybe saw it too now and her eyes began to dart around the workshop, looking, more in hope than expectation, for what Harrington could want. She was not alone as Benjamin found his own gaze wandering over the lines of racks and shelves, that filled every available space not used for machinery and workbenches.

Gothe however had more to say. "I knew your father, Miss Eliza, knew him back years ago. He was, I will say now as I have before, as good a man as I ever met. So if I may ask, if indeed it's not too painful in the telling, how exactly did he die?"

"Eliza?" Benjamin inquired.

"It's my name, Mr West," she told him.

"In that case, it is a pleasure to make your acquaintance, Miss Eliza Maybe." He shook his head slightly in mild bewilderment. As ever, Gothe had been less than forthcoming with nuggets of useful information. He had not even been aware the former manservant knew the former Mr Maybe, let alone that he knew Miss Maybe's name. Occasionally he wondered if Gothe kept things from him on purpose, or if it just never occurred to the former manservant to mention these things. That he did so was a matter of some irritation for Benjamin, if all truths be told. But then Gothe could be a most irritating individual, and the most solid of companions in the same instance, and he found himself wondering, not for the first time in their association, if Gothe had been quite so stoic in life as he was in the post-life state he had been in since before Benjamin had first made his acquaintance. It was one of those things he never felt entirely comfortable asking Gothe about, one of several things…

"Tu-Pa-Ka," the lady said, causing Benjamin to raise an eyebrow, and bring him back to the conversation at hand.

"Eliza Tu-Pa-Ka. Not Maybe, Maybe was just the name my father was known by, not his real name. Europeans have always struggled to pronounce his actual name. So, he seldom used it."

"MaeYaBee Tu-Pa-Ka." Gothe said, which sounded like someone had taken the English language and run it through a mangle to Benjamin's ears, all the stranger for coming from Gothe's lips.

Benjamin saw Miss Maybe's, or Miss Tu-Pa-Ka's eyes, as he corrected himself, light up. A wide genuine smile filling her face. To the surprise of both men she leaned forward, gave the former manservant a quick embrace and planted a tiny kiss on his cheek.

To his utter surprise Benjamin felt a sudden acute pang of jealousy. Gothe for his part took it all without any real change in expression. Though Benjamin would swear that for a passing moment the man's eyes seemed to have a light in them they normally lacked.

"That's exactly right," she said with a remarkably girlish zeal. Then suddenly embarrassed, she pulled away and made to smooth out her clothing, in a vain attempt to hide it. "Forgive me, I've not heard that name spoken aloud since…"

"That's quite alright, Miss Eliza," Gothe said with surprising feeling. "I know what it is to grieve the passing of those we love. I grieve for him myself, though I had not seen him in many years."

Benjamin was more surprised by Gothe's words than anything else he had heard that day. He had seldom heard his former manservant speak with any real passion in his voice. At times he forgot that Gothe was not always as he was now. Perhaps more humanity still clung to the man's hulking frame than he credited.

"That is kind of you to say, Mr Gothe."

"Your father taught me how to pronounce his name correctly when first I met him. Back when we were both serving on the Southern Star. A lifetime ago. Back when, well, when I had a lifetime," Gothe explained to her,

"I'm surprise just how well you learned it," she said.

"Your father offered an incentive at the time," Gothe told her, his voice as deadpan as only the dead can be. "As I recall he promised to stop hitting me when I finally got it right."

The two others stared at him for a moment, then Benjamin, unable to contain his mirth, burst into laughter. Miss Tu-Pa-Ka managed to look shocked for a moment before she too found herself laughing. Benjamin was not sure if it was the absurdly deadpan delivery or just all the tension of the day finally finding some relief, but this struck him as the funniest thing he had heard in an age.

Gothe however looked on unmoved and not for the first time Benjamin found himself wondering if the former manservant's sense of humour had died with him. *Does he even realise the black humour of his words?* Yet in the face of Gothe's stoic expressionlessness the two living people present laughed all the harder, each infecting the other with the desire to do so. So they laughed longer and harder than they should until with some embarrassment the laughter finally petered out.

Once they recovered their collective sensibilities, there was an awkward silence that led Benjamin to speak, as much to bridge the gap as anything else. "My dear Miss Tu-Pa-Ka, I am sorry to press you on this but you were going to tell us how your father died and what part Harrington had in it."

"I was? Yes, I was, wasn't I," Eliza replied to his inquiry, her eyes going wild for a second and sweeping the room, doubtless reminded of the earlier revelation that there must be something in the workshop the odious villain wanted. Then she held Benjamin's eyes a moment, gave a sigh and said, "All right, where do I begin…"

Benjamin pulled a chair over and sat himself down, facing her, "At the beginning is, I have always found, the fashionable place to start," he said, still smiling, which earned him a sharp look that suggested she was trying to decide if he was mocking her or not. But then her eyes softened once more, and she dragged over a seat of her own and with care sat down.

"About a month ago then," she started then paused, for a moment to recall more clearly. "No, it would've been six weeks ago. Yes, that sounds about right, six weeks. Anyway, I came into the workshop and heard my father talking loudly in his office. Not shouting, you understand, he seldom ever shouted, but my father was softly spoken for the most part. When he raised his voice it stood out." She smiled at a memory. "Soft voiced, even after all his years in London. He never quite lost his island accent I think. The language of his people, I learned so little of it as he insisted I speak English all the time, but he spoke it sometimes to me as a child. It's a beautiful language full of soft consonants and gentle verbs. Like, well, I like to think it's like the islands themselves. Words that flow like the rippling tides on the beaches or like a light breeze through the treetops. Among his people only words of war were ever spoken loudly. So you see I knew that if my father was being loud, he was angered by someone or something. And as he was loud that day, I knew something was wrong." A look of regret passed over her features.

"I didn't want to disturb him however, so I made myself busy around the shop and I only heard snatches of their conversation. Something that my father insisted was not for sale, something about him not betraying a trust, something about the west. It didn't mean much…"

She stopped talking suddenly, her gaze falling directly at Benjamin as the proverbial penny dropped into place.

"West? He was not talking about the west at all, was he? It was a name, wasn't it? West. Was he talking... he was talking about you? What hand did you have in this?" she snapped. Anger in her voice and in her eyes too. Anger which Benjamin found disturbing. It had been obvious to him just how much her father's death weighed upon her. But the fire that flashed in her eyes with the mere suspicion he might in some way be involved took him aback. It spoke of violence, reprisal and an inner fury he found hard to attribute to the woman before him. The woman with whom he had been laughing only moments before.

Benjamin raised his hand, palms outward, defensively and shook his head. "No, not me. I wrote to your father no more than two weeks ago. I'd not tried to contact him before then, I'd not had any reason to do so before then, it must have been something else..." A thought occurred to him. "Or someone else... My father and yours knew each other. Your father worked for mine years ago. It would be how Gothe knew your father, and mine, when they sailed on 'The Southern Star'... that was my father's ship, he was their employer. More than that, I believe my father considered yours a friend. In his journals he spoke of Maybe with a great deal of respect, that... Well, that's why I came here today. That's why I sought him out."

The fire in her eyes dimmed but did not quite extinguish. He could tell there was still a spark of suspicion at the back of her mind. Not of him or even of his motives, but that by the proxy of his father he was involved somehow in the events that led to her own father's death. Yet despite her obvious suspicion she gathered herself once more.

"You'll have to explain why you came here, but let's not muddle the story further for now. I'll finish mine first," she said, a cold determination about her demeanour. "As I said, I made myself busy around the shop. I'm not by nature an eavesdropper, just so you understand. As far as I was concerned my father's business was his own. But knowing someone had angered him so... well, I couldn't help but listen. But I heard little more than I've said already. A few minutes after that Harrington came out of the office, telling my father he'd be back in a few days 'if my father wished to reconsider his position'. My father said something to the effect of 'if you wish to waste your time coming back that's your own regard.' And stormed back into the office. He chose not even to take the time to show his guest to the door. That's when I knew just how much trouble there was. You need to understand my father was a courteous man. It wasn't in his nature to not see a guest to the door and then shake their hand before they left. It may seem a trivial thing, but it spoke volumes to me. For my father to be so far off keel, so discourteous, even to a man he had disagreed with... well, it was unusual, let me just say that." She became thoughtful for a moment, absently letting her eyes drift around the workshop that had been her father's domain.

"You knew my father wasn't a native of London?" she asked after a drawn-out silence, and Benjamin nodded despite that having been plain even had he not known Maybe came from other climes.

"Well, native or not my father considered himself a Londoner. As much as any man born here. But he was no fool, he knew fair well there were those who considered him otherwise. Those who would take one look at his islander skin and think him a lesser man. A pagan. A barbarian. A foolish native of some foreign land. Not a man of this fair city," she told them with an undercurrent of distaste in her voice.

Benjamin knew well enough what she was talking about. There were always those who would look down upon anyone not of their class or race or who were just other. He had no trunk with such thinking himself, at least he always hoped he did not. What little he had learned from his father had at least taught him the value of a man had little to do with what you saw on the outside, and everything to do with what was within. But still he knew such sentiments were easy said when your birth was one of privilege, as was his own. Few men of colour moved in his social circles and holding such libertarian beliefs as 'all men are made equal' was far easier to square when you were born more equal than others in terms of wealth and standing. The working classes were, when all is said and done, easy to consider equal in the gaze of the rich man's eye. As such, her words made him a tad uncomfortable, despite how libertarian he thought himself.

Eliza continued… "Just so you know, Maybe is a name known in Cheapside and beyond. A name that has a reputation for being both honest and as straightforward as they come. A reputation that was hard won, but well earned. My father saw to that and knew well its value. He worked hard to maintain the manners and respect of this city. To keep the social niceties no matter what. So no man could point to the colour of his skin and claim he was less than them, though enough have done just that over the years. It was important to him, you understand, important in ways a man born of this city could chose to ignore where he could not. So, for him to not walk a guest to his door. Well… it spoke volumes, that's all I'm saying."

She grew silent once more, Benjamin felt a pang of sympathy for her, she was clearly giving voice to many regrets. He wanted to tell her it was okay, but he knew it was not, so kept his own council and gave her time to tell her story at her own pace. After a moment she continued…

"I didn't ask him any details, and he didn't talk to me of them. But I knew. I knew whatever had happened in that office played on his mind for days. He spent a long hour up there, in his back office." She pointed at the raised mezzanine office that lay up a set of sturdy wooden steps. "But time passed and I dare say he forgot about it and moved on. He was like that whenever someone irked him. No matter what insult had been done. Eventually he would just put it behind him and not let such things cloud his thoughts. But then about three weeks ago Harrington showed up again. This time I was here from the start and I knew there was trouble brewing from the look on my father's face when that skeletal bastard walked in with those two goons of his beside him. The smile that was almost always on my father's face dropped away the moment the swine came through the door, and he gave me a look that suggested I should make myself scarce. But I wasn't going anywhere, my curiosity alone kept me here."

"Understandable…" Benjamin said, which drew a sharp look from her, which softened after a moment when he gave her a sympathetic half-smile.

"I guess my father knew I was going to be stubborn if he insisted. I could never hide such things from him. So, he took the easier option and invited Harrington up to his office, closed the door and left me down here with the goon squad. Whatever went on between them didn't take long. A few minutes later at the most my father flung open the office door and marched Harrington out. Saying he would be damned before he'd sell out to him, and Harrington, well, he looked as angry then as he did just now, but he took his goons and stalked off anyway."

"He wanted to buy this place back then too?" Benjamin interrupted. The idea struck him as an odd one, property in Cheapside was not hard to come by. A great many riverside warehouses and business were run down or abandoned these days. With steam wagons replacing much of the old river trade, the value of riverside warehousing had plummeted.

Eliza shrugged, it clearly making little sense to her either. "So he claimed, lock stock and barrel. Though the way his offer was phrased it was more 'sell out to me or else'. And well… My father wasn't having that, none of it. I've seldom seen him as angry. But he wouldn't explain further, he wasn't a man to share his troubles. All he told me then was that it was all over some map or other and some documents that had been left in his keeping by some old friend. He didn't go so far as to explain who that old friend was and why he was holding them. He just stormed off to his office, telling me he needed to think for a while."

"What map?" Benjamin asked, making no effort to hide his interest.

"I suspect you know, Mr West," Eliza replied sharply, giving him a hard glare, before continuing. "We can get to that though. Let me finish my telling first."

Benjamin nodded in acquiescence but could not hide his impatience. Eliza clearly knew more than she had let on about his reasons for coming to Cheapside as it was clear she had drawn connections between those reasons and what had happened to her father. He tried not to entertain the thought she would take ill against him. A lot rode on him obtaining what he had come to Cheapside for, though now he considered it, he found to his own surprise there were other reasons he would prefer she not take ill against him.

"I think the documents your father held were from mine," he said, and the withering look she gave him suggested she had already reached that conclusion. He held up his palms in surrender to that point and urged her to continue her story.

"Anyway," she said, taking up the tale once more. "A couple of weeks went by, nasty weeks as it turned out. Strange things happened, deliveries got way laid, or held up. An order for some compressor valves from a company my father had traded with for years was cancelled out of the blue. The flue for the steam drill was blocked by a dead seagull and the smoke poured back through. Little things as well, the door was jammed by an abandoned hand cart. People paid late or short for parts my father made. We knew it was all Harrington's doing, stirring things up and trying to convince my father that it would be less hassle to just take his offer. Then after all that, he sent one of his goons around again to repeat the offer with a touch of menace. 'Take it or leave it, but woe on you if you leave it,' was the message."

"Your father took that badly, I take it?" Gothe muttered.

"Of course. He could be stubborn at the best of times. All the more when someone pushed him. He wasn't about to let some dock crawler like Harrington drive him out. I think he expected it would all die down eventually. He was sure once Harrington realised he wasn't going to cave to intimidation, he would back off. My father always did think the best of people and expect the best to happen. He sent Harrington's man away with a flea in his ear and thought that the end of it. And it seemed like it was for the next couple of days. Everything quietened down. It was about then he got your letter, so I suspect he thought once he gave all the documents to you that would be the end of it."

"So, he planned to give me the documents? You knew why I was here to see your father?"

"I did once I put it together, and he did, but I haven't decided yet what I plan to do with them."

"They are mine by right," Benjamin said, keeping his tone even but finding it hard to disguise how irked he felt.

"I'm not sure I care right at this moment whose they are by right. Those letters cost my father his life. For half a crown I might shove the damn lot of them in the furnace. Rather that than let Harrington have them and I'm no surer about you, Mr West, than I am about him," she said, iron in her voice, angry, stubborn iron. A trait he did not have to wonder if she inherited from her father, it was all too clear she had.

"I had no part in his death, Miss Tu-Pa-Ka," Benjamin said firmly, stumbling over the strange name. "Though I can see why you believe Harrington had. I have damn all to do with him and I've no idea what he would want with my father's documents or come to that how he even knows of their existence."

"So, you're telling me your coming here is no more than coincidence?" she snapped back.

"I'm sure it is not, but ask yourself, if your father would have given me the documents happily, why would I have anything to do with Harrington?"

"I…" she started, then wavered for a moment. "I need to be sure is all."

"I understand, but finish your story, tell us what happened to your father. I want to know just how sure you are it was Harrington."

"Why?" she asked, with a plea in her voice, all the emotion and anger of the last few hours rolling over her like waves. "Why bother to finish the story now?"

"Because if he did indeed have a hand in your father's death. Well, then I think we may have to kill him, don't you?" Benjamin replied.

Chapter Six

Gaslight Retrospective

The sound of Bow bells were echoing in the distance, telling him it was midnight. The workshop was dark now save for gaslight from the street filtering in through dirty windows, the light dimmed further by the hazy fog that was rolling in from the riverbank. Just another smog-bound London night, the coal fired heart of the city once again giving birth to its own shroud. A lone oil lamp burned by the door where Constable Riley was dozing against a crate. Up on the gantry, in front of the office, Benjamin stood alone, pushing tobacco into his pipe, contemplating the day that had just passed.

Gothe had retreated to the shadows of the stacks and found somewhere to bed down for the evening. Not that the flesh golem actually slept, as Benjamin understood it, he just sort of switched off. Eliza had retired an hour ago to the small apartment behind the office on the upper floor where she had her own room.

Partly because it was too late to catch a train back west, and partly because their business seemed far from done, Miss Tu-Pa-Ka had given them leave to stay in the workshop for the night. Begrudgingly she had offered him her father's room to sleep in, but Benjamin sensed she was just being polite. Not wishing to impose, he had declined the offer. Besides, the dead man's bed had little appeal if the full truth be told. Particularly after listening to Eliza finish the story of how her father died.

As she told it, a few days after events around the workshop had calmed down, just after dusk, one of the local street boys came running into the workshop. It was a common enough practice to send urchins with messages, so this rang no alarms for her father. He simply asked the boy what his business with him was. The boy explained a steam launch had broken down at Sheers Wharf some quarter of a mile down the embankment. The boat's master had grabbed the boy and sent him to fetch an engineer and pointed him in the direction of Maybe's workshop. All of which was plausible enough, as Maybe's work was well known up and down the river. Besides which the boy knew nothing more than that. Maybe had tipped the lad a ha'penny and smiling to himself, for there was little the man loved more than messing about with engines, he had told Eliza he would be back in an hour or two and that was that. He had grabbed a toolbox with some basic tools and set off into the fog bound, gas lit streets for Sheers Wharf. According to Eliza, even had her father thought for a moment there was a danger this was more than it seemed he would have gone anyway. Maybe Tu-Pa-Ka was a man who put great stock in his own reputation. It would be a cold day indeed before he let fear keep him from a job.

That Maybe had such pride in his work, and indeed had earned the right to such pride, Gothe had affirmed from his own knowledge of the man. That being so, Benjamin accepted it as truth at face value rather than assume it was the rose-tinted spectacles of a daughter's love. Besides it all fitted with what his father's journals had had to say of the south sea islander.

What happened to Maybe next was mostly guess work on Eliza's part. But the sum of it was somewhere between the workshop and Sheers Warf, Maybe had taken a blow to the back of the skull with something blunt and heavy. Thus, struck he had fallen, or more likely been thrown, into old lady Thames herself, and like as not been left for dead. Most stories would end there, Benjamin had no doubt, but Maybe must have had a strong will to survive and managed somehow to do so. In the morning he was found, still alive but unconscious in the mud flats at low tide. A pair of local cockle diggers came across him and recognising the Polynesian engineer, they had rushed him to the workshop, causing quite a stir among the riverside folk, most of whom knew Maybe by sight.

What the blow to the head had failed to do, lungs full of river water and a night's exhausted exposure achieved. Only not quite as suddenly and far from cleanly. Lain in his bed, he took to a fever that had run through him, burned him up and never subsided. The waters of the old lady were filthy as ever and weakened by the blow even as big a man as Maybe was, he could not fight off the sickness. Over three days he lapsed between incoherence and unconsciousness, and never fully regained his faculties. The most she had got out of him as she nursed him through those three torrid days was a single name. 'Harrington'. But that single name was enough.

Eliza had had her suspicions before he whispered that name. The chances of the attack being some random robbery gone wrong were too remote. Mr Maybe was too well known a figure on the Cheapside streets, too well respected, and not to put too fine a point on it, he was built like a brick outhouse. A big man to start with, years of slaving over vice and lathe had only made him bigger and stronger. Only a fool would have tried their luck blackjacking a man the like of Maybe Tu-Pa-Ka. So no, she was certain, there was nothing random about this, even had he never whispered that name, Eliza knew who was to blame for the attack. Well, who had ordered it at any rate. She doubted Harrington would have got his own hands dirty.

On the third day of fitful fevers, the old engineer finally lost the struggle. Passing from the world in fits of agony, as Eliza told it. It was, she said, a terrible way to die. Benjamin found no reason to disagree with that assessment. He felt bile rising at the back of his throat as she described her father's final hours, and even Gothe who could seldom be described as anything other than impassive, showed a degree of emotion Benjamin was unaware the dead man possessed. He almost pitied Harrington if he ever crossed Gothe's path again... Almost.

Harrington, now there was the thing that troubled Benjamin. How could Harrington know of his father's map and papers? As far as he could gather, the man was no more than a gutter gang boss. A big noise in Cheapside, it was true enough, he did not doubt, but beyond that nothing more than a common criminal. That part of it all made little sense. Which worried at West, there must be more to it and someone else in play, someone pulling Harrington's strings, that much he was sure of. But who? Now that was the question.

Benjamin lit his pipe and leaned on the balcony, took a deep draw on the tobacco and contemplated what he knew. All the while resisting the urge to try the handle of the office door. He was aware Eliza Tu-Pa-Ka had locked it when she retired. If, as he hoped, Miss Maybe intended to give him the map and papers eventually, she certainly had showed no intention of doing so tonight. There was, he was all too aware, still little trust between them. While he was sure she knew he was not connected directly with what happened to her father, it was still that map and those papers that lay at the heart of the matter. Their existence would seem to be the reason of her father's untimely demise. So with that in mind, West was not sure he blamed her for her reticence when it came to letting them go. In her position he would be tempted to burn them as well, and damn everyone else who wanted them. It may be that to do so would be an act of petty spite, but spite was another of those faults of his that he was uncomfortably aware of. He could only hope Eliza did not harbour that kind of spiteful resentment towards him. Perhaps, knowing the documents would be going where they belonged, and that in giving them to him she would also be denying them to the odious Harrington, would be enough to convince her to hand them over. They were, after all, his by right. His father's legacy and the hope that perhaps he could finally discover what became of the old man.

Smoking his pipe, there in the darkness of the workshop, he half convinced himself she would see the wisdom of handing them over in the morning. Which pleased him, for all he worried at the possibility he might be wrong. Sooner they be freely given, as was he believed her father's honest intent, than matters become unpleasant. Benjamin West did not think of himself as a man given to enjoying unpleasantness for its own sake.

Benjamin was, however, also entertaining thoughts of the lock picks, the ones secreted in a hidden pocket of his great coat. They would make easy work of the simple tumbler lock to the office door, of that he had no doubt. They were, he would be the first to admit, not the tools of a gentleman, but then he was not always the most reputable of gentlemen. They were one of his little fascinations which were in turn perhaps another of those little faults of his. He had, what his old school masters liked to describe as, the wrong kind of inquiring mind. Which was to say a mind for anything and everything that was not part of the public school curriculum. If there was an activity frowned upon by the school, he would be sure to be engaged within it. In part he knew this was an act of rebellion against his stifling upbringing. He had been a permanent boarder at a string of public schools, ever since he was orphaned at a young age by a father who was considered to be an embarrassment by the rest of the extended West family. By extension Benjamin himself had become something of an embarrassment to them. Seeing to his education was of course the Christian thing to do, indeed they considered it a matter of family honour. But none of his various uncles and aunts wanted the child for the summer, or indeed any direct contact with him. It was not as if they particularly wished to spend time with their own children, that was what you employed governesses for. Woe betide they let the progeny of the family's black sheep into the fold. Ill luck such as that could be a contagion. Better by far to leave him in the care of the public school system. It is what the fees were paid for, after all.

Benjamin had not been alone in this position of course. The public schools of England served as long term boarding for many sons and daughters whose parents were abroad between terms. But for few others was school a permanent purgatory in the days of their adolescence. This upbringing did engender a degree of guile within him however, and a spirit of independence that had served him well in the years since.

Despite the temptation they represented, however, the lock picks remained in their hidden pocket, and the door remained locked. Whatever fragile understanding he may yet achieve with Eliza, he decided against endangering it with a wilful act of transgression. He would sooner see her an ally in whatever game was being played out. Which naturally came down to Harrington again, all be he a criminal of little note in the grander scheme of things. Which still left that question unanswered, just who was pulling the snivelling swine of a man's strings. Benjamin West would have given much right then to know the answer to that little conundrum.

He puffed on his pipe and stared into the dim gloom of the workshop, absently wishing he had some gin to go with the tobacco. All the while wondering what was in the damn papers that were so tantalisingly close now, just beyond the locked office door. Benjamin's knowledge of the documents that had been in Maybe Tu-Pa-Ka's keeping, as he had vouchsafed to Eliza, stemmed from the moment a junior clerk of the family law firm arrived at his door two weeks prior. The clerk had brought with him, of all things, a sealed letter from his father, left in the keeping of the firm some fifteen years before. That in itself had come as a surprise to Benjamin, who had long since resigned himself to knowing no more of his father than what little his family had deemed fit to tell him over the years. Little of which had been forthcoming from positions of high regard.

Yet there in his drawing room on the day of his final majority he was handed a message from a long dead father he had barely known. A man, it may be worth mentioning, that he had long held in some margin of contempt. The resentment he felt towards that long absent paternal figure, source of all the woes he had endured in his youth, had a hard grip upon him. It left him with little love and less respect for the shadowy spectre that his father had been in his life. As a child, of course, he had defended his father's name in the face of those who mocked. West, the famous failure, the explorer who found nothing. West, the villain who swindled investors into his mad schemes and left nothing but unpaid dividends, and notes of owing. More than one of his schoolmates had been the scions of a family who had invested sums in West senior's adventuring. Boys whose fathers no doubt took a certain delight in warning their sons to have no doings with the West boy. One of the masters of his last school had lost a hundred pounds by investing in West's last great expedition to the Amazon basin. Benjamin suspected that the master had taken unwarranted glee in extracting those pounds back in the flesh of the West junior's backside. By his later school years he had long since ceased to defend his father's name, wishing in truth that he could rid himself of his ignoble patronage.

University had changed that resentment to a degree. He had taken the classics more out of spite than anything else, when an uncle he had never met wrote to him with instructions to study something 'of use.' He did however spend a great deal of time in the university library, between bouts of drunkenly trying to learn the secrets of life from the barmaid's apron. It was almost by chance a friend stumbled upon something which was to change Benjamin's opinion of his father. It was, of all things, a relatively new map of the world, only three years out of date, which contained, among other new additions to older maps, the small string of islands in the deep Pacific named The West Islands. His friend had found the name amusing enough to point it out to him. It was after all an odd moniker for a chain of islands in the middle of the great eastern ocean. Amused, they set out to find the origins of the name and were surprised to learn the little chain of islands had actually been discovered by his father. Hence, they had in fact been named for him.

To Benjamin this was a redemption of sorts, for all his childhood indignities. It was proof after all that his father was more than a failure. In a fever of investigation, he tried to read all he could find on The West Islands of the Pacific. Which turned out to be next to nothing. In all the libraries of Oxford he found little reference to the islands beyond the odd note in a geographic paper to do with their discovery and the claiming of them for the crown by 'Sir Edward West in 1806'. It took a trip to London and the British Library to find anything more illuminating. Though slightly more illuminating would prove to be the appropriate vernacular. After several requests for all information regarding the islands before his visit, and two days of waiting upon his arrival, one of the librarians emerged from the lower stacks with a dusty filing box. In this unassuming repository was held the sum total of all knowledge of The West Islands within the British Library's hallowed halls of knowledge.

This depository of knowledge consisted of a few hand drawn maps of the five islands themselves of reasonable but undistinguished quality. A larger map of the chain in its entirety, and a final map charting the Pacific as a whole, marking the location of the islands. There was also a handwritten set of notes of dubious handwriting, from which Benjamin derived the pertinent facts.

The island chain was isolated in the extreme, a thousand miles from anywhere in all directions. The largest island a few scant miles across and home to an active volcano from which the islands had sprung in the first place. They lay in the path of no prevailing currents, far from the trade winds, in a place where no ships had any great reason to pass. The population of the island was none. Agriculture none. Plant life, various unremarkable specimens which never got back to Britain. Animal life, none to speak of. Bird life limited. Rare minerals none. Value, insignificant to none. Indeed, one witty commentator from the foreign office had added a note saying that the addition of The West Islands to the realms of Her Majesty's Empire succeeded only in lowering the average value of land within it by its square footage.

As an episode for most this would have been disheartening. To find his father's only discovery of note was a chain of islands that were of no worth. However, it became a point of pride for him. A perverse pride that Benjamin had revelled in. There is a difference, he had come to think, in being told your father was a failure and knowing that it was true. His father had failed as the great explorer he set out to be. But he had failed grandly. If nothing else there was one tiny begotten spot of land on the globe which would forever hold his name. A place which he had discovered. The West Islands. Named for him and him alone. That was an achievement in itself, even if they proved to be of no actual value.

A few years later, on a night's carousing to celebrate the end of finals, university about to be all but behind them all, he was with a loose collection of what could almost be called friends. Robert Farnsworth, who would not have made it on to even the loosest of lists of those friends, had pointed out loudly, "The main reason no one had ever discovered the West Islands before was probably because they weren't worth discovering." An observation for which he received a roar of laugher at Benjamin's expense. Farnsworth had warmed to his subject, and went on with his diatribe, "Hell, they have probably been discovered on several occasions by those who did not think they were even worth mentioning. Cook probably sailed past them, thought better of it on his way to discover Australia." Farnsworth, who had a position waiting for him in the Foreign Office, thanks to a father in the service, considered himself a member of the ministry already, and as such took great delight in repeating the quote of the witty official from the dusty box, in order to complete Benjamin's embarrassment.

When Benjamin took residence in his father's long mothballed house in Kensington a few weeks later he had done little but use it as a place to sleep. Then, a year after taking up residence he had received that letter from the distant past, via the family solicitor. By then he was once more far from enamoured of his father, and so the letter itself had lain undisturbed for several days on the dusty desk. Gothe, who had in a strange way come with the house, had proved unenlightening. So, it was not until his curiosity finally got past the walls of resentment that Benjamin read his father's letter.

The letter, and its contents, had sparked a renewed interest however, and he had launched into a week of frantic activity, reading and sorting his father's papers. The note had seemed both simplistic and cryptic. The essence of it being. 'Seek Maybe, he has the map and notes.' It took a day to find out who Maybe was and exactly where he resided. Then there were the final words in the letter, words which had taken on new meaning to Benjamin in the last few hours. A strange final instruction from father to son regarding Maybe's daughter. One which he struggled to believe was meant literally…

All of which led to the questions which troubled him now on the balcony overlooking the workshop. What was this mysterious map, what of the notes? Why had his father left a message for him to receive on his twenty fifth birthday that was so damn cryptic? What was it that someone knew that he didn't? Knowledge that led them to such lengths to get hold of the map before him? Mystery piled on mystery, and he had to presume, someone, somewhere, was pulling the strings. If nothing else it was at least something, something to break out of the sterile routine of life he had dropped into. The curse of being independently wealthy, living on the income of investments laid down before he was born, was boredom. He was self-aware enough to know there were many scraping a living in the slums of the nation who would envy him his boredom. His occasional forays to the seedier side of London taught him that much, and there had been more than one of those. So, if nothing else at least his investigation into this strange legacy was definitely not proving to be dull.

He drew on his pipe once more, as the echoes of the bells fell away into the night and he found himself contemplating the error in turning down the dead man's bed. Propping himself against the wall to sleep sitting up held little appeal. He would have considered trying to find a local hostelry for the night, but he suspected the flea pits of Cheapside would be less agreeable than sleeping in the workshop. Despite his reticence, he knocked the dying embers of the pipe tobacco out and sat himself on the balcony floor, his back to the office wall. Pulling his great coat around himself like a blanket, he closed his eyes and tried vainly to find some sleep. A listless hour passed of half dozing before, finally, he started to succumb to his tiredness.

Just as he was finally dropping to sleep he half heard the sound of a key turning in a lock, and the creak of the office door being opened. Later he would swear he saw Eliza Tu-Pa-Ka tiptoe past him, but if that was half a dream or a real memory he could not say. In any event he soon fell into a fitful sleep.

Chapter Seven

An Inking of Night

Living in Cheapside you got used to working the occasional odd hours. As an artist, which Fredricks considered himself to be, normal hours were always a matter of speculative debate. All the same being woken at one in the morning by someone braying on the shop door was somewhat unusual. His normal response, if normal could be considered the right word for such an event, would have been to pick up something heavy and be ready to swing it once he opened the door. He was in the process of doing just that when he recognised the voice that accompanied the braying. Fighting with a matchbox, he lit a hand lamp and made his way downstairs into his shop and studio.

"Eliza?" he said gruffly while pulling the bolt on the heavy wooden door of his shop. "Miss Maybe… What in Neptune's name are you wanting at this time of night?" Most anyone else would have gotten the sharp end of his tongue and be told to sling their hooks for waking him at such an hour. His fire long gone to ash, the room was cold and his breath added to the mist that curled through the door as he opened it.

"Fred, I've need of your skills," Eliza replied, bustling through the door.

He sighed to himself and shut it behind her, but not before taking a second to look up and down the fog bound street beyond. A young woman out in a peasouper like that could attract undesirable types, and he was not unduly worried she might have been followed.

The door closed and he took a moment to peer at the girl, wondering what had dragged her to his door… "At this time of night? Look, Miss, you know I have nothing but respect for you, girl. Your father was always a fine friend to me, so he was, and even after that business with… well, enough said. You know you're always welcome in my shop but what on earth brings you to it at this time of night?"

"This," she said, then held up a faded piece of paper. Heavy old paper, of the kind he rarely saw, mainly because it was poor quality by the standards of the day. But it was old, very old by the look of it. It seemed to be a map of some kind, and full of words he could not understand. Not that he could have understood many of them if they were English, his grasp of the written word was minimal. There were some he knew well, they cropped up often enough in his work that he had learned to recognise them. The words on the map did not look English at all however, the hand it was written in was old as well.

She held it up to the light so he could see it better and told him, "I need it copied, and I need it copied tonight."

"I don't even know what half of this means," he lied, having no desire to admit the extent of his ignorance.

She smiled at him, her face doing that same trick she used to do when she was a little one asking for sweet money while her father was talking shop. The look she had that, in his opinion, turned a plain girl into a beauty he found hard to disappoint.

"I would have been surprised if you did, Fred, it's old Spanish. I don't understand the words myself. But I know you can copy them perfectly; you've an eye for that."

What lay behind the flattery in her words was not lost on him, but his pride would not let him believe it was merely that. If he had any real talent, he was aware it was his ability to redraw things with perfect detail. A gift to a man in his profession, indeed more so to one in his other profession, the one of which he seldom spoke. Place any original document before him and he could reproduce it. A skill which was occasionally employed for less than honest work, but needs must, and he had need to pay his rent once in a while if business in his more honest craft had been slow.

"Well I guess that's true," he replied with false modesty which fooled her not a lick he was sure.

"You know it's true," she said and gifted him another smile.

He was, he knew, of an age to be her father, but that smile reminded him of a time when he was not.

"And you need this tonight?" he asked, though in truth he was already running his fingers over ink bottles in the racks that lined one wall, picking out the right ones for the job.

"I do. It's a matter of some urgency," she said with a note of pleading in her tone which he was not sure he believed. He knew Eliza had a manipulative streak to her at times. But he had little objection to being manipulated by pretty girls, even if they were like a daughter to him.

"It's not the normal thing," he noted. For several years he had being making copies of engineering designs for Eliza's father. He never understood those either but did not feel the need to. Generally, they were borrowed designs that Maybe had to return. Almost always a rush job of some kind, and occasionally Fredricks suspected that was due to Mr Maybe not being entirely at liberty to have them copied. Occasionally large engineering firms might farm something out to small workshops like Maybe's, but they would demand the return of the diagrams and drawings once the work was complete. Maybe, well, he was the kind of man who had a passion for his craft not unlike Fredricks' passion for his own, so with Maybe when it came to engineering diagrams, it was like a magpie collecting shiny things. Fred Fredricks was not a man to overly burden himself with the motives of those who employed his talents, however, so long as he was being paid he would copy anything he was asked to copy and let the right of it be a question for the other man's conscience.

"No, it's not, and paper won't do for this. I need a more permanent record, something that can't be taken from me," Eliza said, walking towards the back of the shop, where a long-padded table lay.

"Oh," Fredricks said surprised. A late-night visit for his more illicit work was not all that unusual, but one for his stock and trade, that was unusual by any standards. He sniffed and considered what she was asking him to do. "You want all that done tonight…? All of it… that's a hell of a lot in one go, girl."

"I know, Fred, I know, but I need you to do it all the same," she replied, and the determination in her voice convinced him, if not of the wisdom of doing so, but that she would not be foiled in her desire. That set his mind. There were others who could do the work, but he would be damned before someone else worked on that canvas this night.

He grabbed his ink and the small case of needles from the counter as she herself lay face down on his table.

In the darkness of a doorway opposite the small tattooist shop, a corpse stood watching. The dead are seldom surprised, at least that was true of Gothe. He suspected, in so much as he suspected anything, that the majority of the dead were never surprised by anything on account of them being dead, which for most is a very final experience. As it should have been for him. He wondered, on occasion, when he wondered anything, if they were the lucky ones.

The fog from the river was cold. An icy chill in the air that he felt not at all, but still shivered. The memory of cold was enough. That's all he was, he knew, memories. Memories of a man who died some fifteen years past.

Memories that walked about under their own steam, but just memories all the same.

As such, he remembered a promise to a dead man, this one fully dead and buried but a few hours before. An old promise that man had probably long forgotten and knowing that man would not hold him to this night. But if all that he was, was a collection of memories, then Gothe would hold true to those memories as well as he could. He had taken a bullet for them in the graveyard, but that did not end his commitment. The last time he had seen Maybe's child before this day she had been three years old, and he had been a living man. Maybe's words to him were the fruits of a friendship hard won, and of the kind often spoken when two old friends meet.

"If anything ever happens to me, look out for her, Gothe, if you're able," Maybe had said a few days before the Southern Star left on her final voyage. A foolish request of a man bound for south America from a man staying in London for the love of his wife and child.

"While there's breath in my body," Gothe had replied at the time. Ironically there was no real breath there now, as he strove to fulfil that promise. Gothe did not think in terms of irony, however.

A couple of months after that conversation, Gothe had died in the Caribbean and for a short time he had rested. It had been a stupid death, one caused by drinking the local gut rot and offending the wrong crowd. He had died leaving a gambling debt, one that was collected on his soul. Some men are of a nasty breed, particularly the ones that own plantations, want cheap labour, and know a mix of voodoo and ancient Hebrew magic. So, he had laboured on a debt a bundle of memories trapped behind a compulsion to labour. Had he been of a philosophical bent he might have said that made him as human as the next man. But the dead have little need for philosophy.

His freedom was won when his memories were stronger than the compulsions laid upon him and he escaped, memories of promises made. Promises made to Maybe, promises made to Benjamin's father, promises he had failed in life, which he would not fail in death. For in the end without his memories and promises what was he but a corpse that did not know when to lay down.

And so, he watched the shop front, not wondering what was happening within, that did not matter to him, all that mattered was the promise to keep her safe.

A small spark within him, which some religions would have perhaps named as his soul, had thoughts of its own. That spark helped him keep up the pretence of personhood and hope. It wondered if it may one day rise once more to the surface. But for now, it was content, for what's the use of hope to the dead.

A half mile away in the doorway of the workshop Constable Riley was snoring happily and failing utterly in his duty as guard. His snores reverberated through the workshop and disturbed Benjamin enough to wake him. He was about to shout down to the man when there was a thud and the snoring suddenly stopped. Later Benjamin could remember thinking at the time that the constable must have turned over in his sleep and knocked something over. As such he pulled his coat tighter around him and huddled down to seek a few more hours rest.

Had he known the workshop better and been more used to the surroundings he might have felt some alarm when he heard heavy boots on the stairs. He half-heartedly assumed Gothe was moving about as the man had wont to do of a night and in his dozing state it barely registered with him until it was too late that there was more than one pair of boots on the stairs.

Suddenly, before he had time to get to his feet or mount any form of defence he was being grabbed by a pair of big hands and proceeded to take a blow to the head. Then laying semi-conscious on the floor, he took a couple of boots to the ribs for good measure before being left rolling in agony as a couple of thick set thugs, brought along as much for their ability to open doors as close eyes, set about battering down the office door. He hardly heard the men who employed them casually strolling up the stairway while this exercise was undertaken.

In the blur that was all that remained of his vision and the haze of his remaining consciousness, Benjamin recognised one of the men as the skeletal thin Harrington. The other he also knew, though he had difficulty placing him for a moment. Yet without any real awareness of what he was saying he muttered the second man's name

The last thing he heard was a refined home counties accent which said to him, "Why, West, what an unwelcome surprise to find you here." Then the speaker punctuated his words by giving Benjamin another far from friendly kick to the stomach as he finally lapsed from consciousness completely.

Chapter Eight

A Soul in a Bottle

"Well, that's it all done, Miss Eliza. I hope you're happy with it because it's going to be with you a long time," Fredricks said, his voice sounding as tired as he felt.

"I hope so, Fred, I really do," she replied, smiling despite the pain he knew she must be feeling. He felt troubled by her words. They seemed too fatalistic for a woman so young. A woman well known for her smile and her cheerful nature. She like her father had been a fixture in Cheapside for many years. Seeing the pair walking the streets was a welcome sight that could lend cheer to a dull day. It was sad to think that her father would no longer tip his hat when he passed by and grin that broad grin of his. *A damn shame how he passed*, he caught himself thinking, hoping Eliza was not going to go the same way any time soon.

Outside the sun was rising, burning away the last of the night's river fog. His hand ached from the repetitions of his art. Surveying his work from above, he was still not entirely sure what to make of it. It was not his finest work, of that he was sure. Which was not to say he had done less than his best. But a work of art it was not. It was however as an exact copy of the map as it could be in so much as it could be repeated on a human canvas. He had missed no detail, added no flourish. It was just what had been requested.

"Damnedest thing I've ever been asked to do," he muttered, as she struggled to sit up, cramp from long hours just laying still no doubt burning at her. He did not envy her that. It was a longer session than he had any right to inflict, but if she was not going to complain then he wasn't going to complain about the ache in his wrist, or his eyes burning. "The damnedest thing…" he said again, a little louder perhaps than he intended.

"And yet I'm going to ask you forget you ever did it," she said to him quietly but with a harder edge to her voice than he had ever heard her use before.

Fredricks laughed, a slightly bitter laugh of self-knowledge. "You need have no fear of that, lass. Not sure I'd want anyone to know that was my work. Not sure I wish to know myself. So have no fear. I aren't going to be saying nothing to no one."

Eliza granted him a smile as she shuffled her shoulders and pushed her dress back over them. The smile turned to a wince as a shot of pain hit her and Fred grimaced. All Eliza did however was snort a breath and set herself up straight, that wince the closest to recognising the pain she had shown.

"I know that, Fred. I trust you to your word, always will. But I need to ask you a couple more favours before I leave," she said to him.

"If you've a need of something, ye can ask I'm sure," he told her, though there was a note of hesitation in his voice. He was not sure what she was mixed up in and given what he had just spent the bulk of the night doing, he was not sure he wanted to be drawn further into it. He was just as sure it was most likely stuff she was better off out of herself. Way her father died… well, everyone knew it wasn't right what happened. He did not want anything like that happening to her, but more than that, he did not want any such thing happening to him either.

"Oh… Don't look so worried, Fred. I just need to borrow a pair of scissors for a minute," she said.

He relaxed and opening a drawer he handed her an old but sharp pair. He was not entirely surprised she carefully cut six inches off the bottom of the map and threw the cut off section on the smouldering fire. He had no idea what the words on it had said, even had they been in English he would have struggled to recall exactly how they were formed. He guessed she did, or knew they were important enough to have only one copy, one kept close to hand. She was sly he would give her that. Whatever she was up to, she was playing a long game, and he was more willing than ever to forget all he knew of it.

Thinking this, he watched the smouldering paper catch the flame and flare up, an odd green colour to the flame they produced, probably down to whatever ancient ink was on the paper. After it was burned away, he turned back to Eliza as another thought struck him. "You said two favours?" he inquired, worried what the second might be.

"Well yes, there is a second thing... Could you do me up?" she said and smiled again, motioning over her shoulder to the tie ribbons on the back of her dress.

Fredricks grimaced again. This was definitely going to hurt. He did not envy her that pain at all...

Gothe watched from the early morning shadows as she left the tattooist's and started back towards the workshop. He was in little doubt she was hoping to get back there before anyone else was awake. She had a furtiveness about her gait, and something else he struggled to be sure of. She was in pain of some kind. Which may have struck him as odd had he wished to contemplate why that might be. But the dead seldom contemplate.

He let her get a little way ahead of him before he emerged from the shadows of the doorway in which he had spent the night. Slowly with purpose, he followed her through the waking streets, losing sight of her only when she passed around corners as he hung back. He was not concerned when this happened, he knew where she was heading after all.

It was the third such corner that he rounded to come face to face with a derringer.

As unemotional as only the dead can be, he merely stopped walking, stood there and looked straight down the barrel.

"Good morning, Miss Eliza," he said simply and other than standing his ground he was no more threatening than a lump of rock.

"You're following me," she said, which was a plain statement of fact. One to which he saw no reason to respond to, but he nodded anyway. "Did your master send you to spy on me, Mr Gothe?" Her arm, he noticed, was shaking slightly, though he did not think the gun that heavy.

"My master, Miss?" he enquired.

"Mr West. I take it he is your master?" There was anger in her tone which had little to do with being followed. It was a sharper anger, one of affront. He assumed this was because she disliked masters. As a lady of colour, she might well have reason to do so, even in a cosmopolitan place like London. That was something Gothe could understand.

"No, Miss Eliza."

"No?" she snapped. "No, he did not send you or no, he is not your master?"

"Both, he did not entreat me to follow you, nor is he my master," Goth said, which gained him a look of measured disbelief.

For a moment there was silence between them. A stalemate of words, while the gun remained pointed at him. He was not unduly moved; he was aware should she pull the trigger he could avoid the bullet if he chose. She was not aware of this fact of course, but that seemed unimportant. Her vexed look remained however, so feeling more explanation was required he chose to break the silence.

"I am my own master, Miss Eliza. Following you was a choice I undertook to ensure your safety. Mr West was unaware I did so."

"My safety? Do you think I need a guardian? What interest have you in my safety, Mr Gothe? What, for that matter, makes you think I'd wish your protection?" she asked him, indignation in her voice and a deep-seated anger at the suggestion.

"You have my apology, Miss Eliza. I have, erred, clearly. I sought only to make sure no harm came to you."

"Just why do you imagine I should trust your words, Mr Gothe? You are, and forgive my bluntness, not even among the living as I understand it. Which frankly I do not. You follow me in secret when I'm about my own business. You claim to seek me no harm, but I'm far from convinced of that, as I'm far from convinced you're not Mr West's creature. Mr West, whose business, it seems to me, got my father bloody killed. Do you see therefore why I may not want you following me, Gothe? Do you?"

Gothe remained impassive, and after a moment the gun in her hand waivered slightly. Then as a baker's boy carrying fresh loaves on a tray rounded the corner, she snapped her arm down to her side. The derringer, Gothe noted, retracted into the sleeve of her dress. He was surprised, in so much as he was capable of surprise, that he had not noticed the contrivance before. The gun was mounted on some form of spring-loaded steel rod, which explained how it had come to hand so quickly in the graveyard the day before.

The baker's boy passed, unaware of the tension between them, grumbling to himself about some minor slight or other he had received that morning. As he passed, Eliza stepped closer to Gothe, closing the distance between them so she could keep her voice of even tone and be heard clearly. "In short, Mr Gothe, I've no reason to trust you and will not have you following me, so I bid you desist. If not, well, I will have little compunction in shooting another hole in you. Is that clear?"

Gothe remained silent, torn between two compulsions, the need to watch over Maybe's daughter and the need to honour her wishes. It did not sit well with him that these were at odds. He believed such compulsions were the core of his existence. Without them he had no purpose, and a purpose was something he required. He acted as Benjamin West's man out of the compulsion to serve the son as he had served the father. But this compulsion alone was not enough, not that he could articulate why. He knew only that his autonomy was dependent upon purpose. Without purpose he was nothing but a corpse and would cease to be. That he could decide upon that purpose himself made little difference, the need remained within him.

"I said, do you understand me, Mr Gothe?" she repeated after a few moments had gone by with no answer. Moments he could not account for, which happened whenever he faced such conflicting drives. Blank spots in his consciousness. Moments of nothingness, of being, so he believed, truly dead… Her question brought him back once more.

"I believe so, Miss Eliza," he said with arid dryness. Then a thought, that rarest of things, occurred to him. "You do not trust that I act in your interests, or that I am free to do so. You believe I am a creature driven by the will of others. Others whom you do not trust."

"That's one way to put it… And I will not have it, Mr Gothe. I insist you cease to pay regard to my safety unless I ask you to do so. Which I shall not be doing," she said firmly, with a degree of petulance to her tone.

Gothe held her gaze, then reached down and slowly undid the buttons on his heavy coat, aware as he did so that she was watching him with suspicion. Her hand, which had so recently held her concealed derringer flexed as she made a fist, then stretched her fingers. He was sure she was unaware she was doing so, a nervous action, one of someone on edge, ready to spin out her gun once more. He continued all the same, reaching into the coat and through the waistcoat beneath to a metal plate fixed by screws that went into the bones of his rib cage. He saw her eyes widen slightly when she saw it, and widen still further when he pulled back the latched section of the plate that sat over the cavity above his heart where it lay. She looked ready to bolt at any moment. Not that he would have blamed her if she had. Few people go around reaching into their own bodies, after all. It is not a sight that many are prepared for. Yet despite this she stood firm, fascinated as much as the sight clearly unnerved her.

Gothe reached in and he drew it out. As he did so he felt that same distant feeling the moment it was removed. His sight grew misted as if the fog of the night before had returned, and he felt cold, so cold, the chill of the grave…

He pulled it free and let the latched plate close over the cavity. The it in question was a small glass bottle, of the type a doctor may use for pills or some medicine of another kind. Within it was a pale blue liquid which seemed to glow with unnatural luminescence. The bottle was stoppered with a cork pushed tightly in. As tight as the day it was first sealed some fifteen years before. Red wax had been melted over it to form a permanent seal. The glass itself was thick and heavy despite the smallness of the bottle. The liquid within, which filled it completely, was no more than a thimble full in volume. His eyes, which had never left her, noticed hers following the bottle as he brought it free of the heavy coat. He stretched out his hand, offering her the bottle.

She shook her head. Her eyes wide, her face as pale as it got, she was clearly unnerved and wary of the object. It was a reaction he had witnessed before, though he rarely brought the bottle forth. People were instinctively repelled by it. Feared it. He offered her it again all the same.

"What is it?" she asked. Captivated despite her revulsion. He wondered if she suspected, perhaps she did. It was the kind of thing that appeared within the pages of a penny dreadful. Its light held a fascination to the living that was preternatural, they felt an inner sense of what it was, along with a recognition that seeing it in this way was wrong. They felt drawn to it and repelled at same time.

"My soul," he replied with candour. "And the one that holds it holds my will." He added, then offered it to her once more.

She shook her head. Unwilling to take it or even to touch it.

"You trust me not, I understand that, so I offer you this to show you can trust me. If you hold this, the repository of my soul, then I serve you. For I must serve the bearer of this bottle, it is what I am. It is all that I am," he explained, his voice colder, more distant than usual. As he knew it would be.

For a second she almost reached for the bottle, her hand edging towards it. The temptation to take it, and in doing so to take control was strong. In that moment she wanted to do so, to become the mistress of him, that was clear in her eyes. She desired it, perhaps only because when you have so little control over your own life, to control another so completely is a temptation so hard to resist. For a fleeting second he was sure she would take it and knew then that he would welcome her doing so. Welcome her freeing him of all compulsions save that which she lay upon him. It was a freedom in a way, a different freedom, for he was freely choosing his mistress. Perhaps, he considered, that was the purest of freedoms. Freedom from yourself... From consequence…

She pulled back her hand, a new resolution in her eyes. A decision made, the same decision another had made only weeks before.

"No, Gothe, you keep your bottle. But know I shall trust you for now," she told him in a voice that suggested her words were true.

He closed his hand and reached back under his coat to the latched metal plate above his heart. Setting his soul back in his body and feeling his connection to it grow strong once more. The warmth that had fled returned to him. Yet he found he was disappointed all the same.

In so much as the dead are ever disappointed by anything.

The workshop looked like the fabled ghost locomotive had passed between its walls, becoming corporeal for those few seconds it passed within. Racking had been pulled over, spilling all manner of nuts and bolts and other things over the floor. The furness door hung from one hinge, ashes spilled across the flagstones, drums of oil and other more noxious things were upturned or punctured. Tool rails were bent or broken, their contents scattered. The office door lay halfway down the steps to the mezzanine. The front door itself hung, half-heartedly swinging in the breeze. Eliza and Gothe stepped through it, into the shattered remains of the once orderly workshop, a cold rage settling on Eliza, while Gothe, stood beside her taking stock of the mess, the dead man's stoic silence doing nothing to quell the outrage she felt.

"Blimey, I thought it was just one door. This is a bigger job than I expected," said a local London voice as its owner entered through the broken doorway behind them.

Eliza turned on him, bringing up her arm with a snap, the derringer snapping from her sleeve, the cold rage within turning hot now she had someone to focus it upon.

"Sweet Jesus," the man cried, his hands flying up, and the toolbox he had been carrying crashing to the ground.

Eliza, her full fury focused in her stare, looked at the man before her, and for a moment her finger itched to pull the trigger. Then recognition came to her eyes and the hot fury fled before it.

"Oh, Mr Jefferies. I do apologise, whatever must you think of me," she said, recognising the local carpenter. She relaxed, lowering her arm and letting the derringer slide back home into her sleeve as if it was never in her hand at all. She was still furious but had hold of her temper for the moment at least.

Jefferies lowered his hands uncertainly, taking off his cap in the process and mopping his brow as he did so. A small well-fed man, he was perspiring more than he perhaps should in the cool morning air. It was clear to her he was feeling unsure what to make of the woman and her hulking companion before him. Eliza felt a pang of guilt, she had known Jefferies for years, she used to play with his daughters on the riverbank not so many years ago. Finding himself staring down the barrel of a gun held by the girl who used to tramp home with his children covered in mud, while his wife declared they were the bane of his existence and he laughed with them, was probably not the sort of thing he expected to happen to him that morning.

"That's okay, Miss Maybe," he managed to splutter then replaced his cap and recovered his toolbox. While his gaze took in the mess of the workshop, he put the toolbox down again carefully. Hooking one thumb in his belt he sucked air in over his teeth in the way of workmen everywhere. "I see the old bill made a mess of your dad's shop, heavy handed buggers," he added.

Eliza found herself smiling as she saw the gleam in the man's eyes. She could guess what was going on in his mind, builders and engineers have much in common. He was doubtless considering estimates, time plus material and maybe a little more on top if the police were footing the bill. She found she could not resent him his avarice, doubtless for him there was money to be made tidying up the mess. She was pleased that all her troubles would be doing someone some good at least.

"Not the police," Gothe said with his stoic nuance of tone.

The carpenter was clearly not listening however, he was instead walking slowly around the workshop floor avoiding the worst of the detritus and scribbling notes in a small notebook. With the occasional pause to suck on his pencil and tut loudly.

"No, it wasn't," Eliza murmured and picked her way to the office steps.

Gothe followed slowly behind. There was the odd splatter of blood on the floor, someone bleeding had been marched or dragged across the workshop. It took no great leap of imagination to guess its origin. The stairs at least were mostly clear but the balcony bore the signs of a struggle, though a one sided one. The office doorway was a splintered wreck, the door ripped from its hinges. She stepped through the shattered portal into her father's office. Invoices and other paperwork were scattered everywhere, mingled with engineering drawings pulled from cabinets at random then discarded. Drawers lay broken or cast aside. The main desk had been upturned. Several small models her father had taken great pride in lay smashed to ruins on the floor.

Eliza noticed her face felt wet, and she realised she was crying, crying for the first time since her father died. Somehow, she found herself on her knees in the middle of the shattered ruins of her father's office. Somehow it all brought it home to her.

Her father was gone.

He would never sit behind his great desk again. Smiling, playing with his plans and models, or scowling over the accounts for that matter.

The tears she had held back for days flooded out. She wept.

Behind her in the doorway Gothe stood, silently watching, waiting for the moment to pass, no matter how long it took. Letting her deal with her grief as she must.

For if the dead understand anything, it is grief.

Chapter Nine

Dusk Sheers all Hopes

Light was fading as the sun dropped below the rooftops. Mist was already rising from the river as the temperature dropped. Lamplighters were doubtless walking the streets with their long wick poles, putting flame to gas to light the city in the coming gloom. The streets would still throng with the passage of the day. Hawkers would be shouting out their wares before the markets closed, billboard-men calling out the late headlines to entice the passers-by to buy their half-penny broadsheets. Street life would be bustling in Cheapside as it ever did. Ragamuffins and cutpurses mixed with dockworkers and factory men heading home from long days. The great heaving mass of Londoners were going about their business. But there was nothing but an eerie silence where Eliza stood.

There had been a note. A note pinned to the door that led to the family chambers with a screwdriver hammered through the wood. It read 'Sheers Wharf, dusk'. Three simple words. It did not say why, then the why was obvious. It did not say what to bring, that too was obvious. Despite all the destruction they had unleashed on the workshop, they had not found what they were looking for as Eliza had it in her possession. Which is how she came to be there, of all places, standing before the very dockside where her father had met the blow that was to end his life.

The stoic Gothe, who had remained monosyllabic throughout the process of trying to bring order to the chaos that had been sown, was at her side, as the day grew dim.

Reading the note, she had almost broken down again. Gothe had appeared silently in the doorway and interceded. At some point, while she had been weeping, he must have gone down the stairs and managed to find a kettle. Somehow among the detritus of the workshop he had recovered two cups of fine china and the old worn teapot. He even managed to find a woollen rag to wrap the teapot in as a makeshift cosy. Despite herself, when he had appeared holding a tea tray, she had almost broken into laughter. There was something so mundane and yet ridiculous that in all the destruction that had been wrought, the former manservant had performed that most English of rituals. As if no matter what had happened, a cup of India's finest leaves, dried and then brewed with boiling water could somehow start to put things right. It was not until she was sitting, having righted a chair, the tray perched on an upturned file box, sipping at the warming brew, that she realised it was true.

The remainder of the day was spent sorting out the mess, slowly returning the workshop and her father's office to order. The private quarters had remained untouched for the most part. A few books and papers had been scattered in her father's room. Her own had half-heartedly been ransacked. She surmised that they, whoever they had been, had not wanted to waste time. They held a hostage now after all. Better, they had doubtless reasoned, to make her bring them what they wanted. Clearly, they did not want to waste the night searching for something that could be hidden anywhere. Besides which there was always a chance that the police might stumble by, which probably motivated them not to dally too long. The Bow Street Runners may not be held high in regard in Cheapside, the local bobbies known to take the odd shilling to look the other way, but having one of their own take a tap on the head was not something they would likely let slide. They had taken enough of a chance taking Constable Riley as well as West.

There was however no doubting the intent of the note. They were to bring the map and journals to Sheers Wharf at dusk or like as not the two men would go in the river. Just as her father had.

The joiner had set about his business, repairing the door and in the process managed to dissuade a lacklustre constable from entering the workshop. Presumably he assumed if the joiner was there then he did not need to replace Riley, who must be off on his heels and snoring the day away. Eliza was happy enough to avoid getting the police involved. Things were murky enough without further complication.

She had recovered the journals from the locked trunk below the false bottom of her wardrobe, silently pleased that she had hidden it there the night before. Then she had sent Gothe to Fredricks with instructions to copy as much of the journals as he could then return them to the workshop by five. Gothe had asked no questions, he had seen the note, so she assumed he felt no need to question her actions. She was glad. His stoic resolve to just get on with things gave her something solid to cling on to.

By the time the journal was returned by Fredricks himself, with a sheave of notes, the day was moving on and some semblance of normality had been returned to the workshop. She had thanked him with a handful of coins, a kiss on the cheek and then waved his questions away before returning to the trunk in her wardrobe and locking the copies away.

As she strode out with the left-handed copy of the device she wore on her right wrist and sat at her father's now righted desk, fastening the straps that held the spring-loaded armature to her arm. Gothe entered with another tray of the ever-flowing tea. Without questioning her, he placed it carefully on the desk and poured her a cup.

"It's going to be dangerous," he said, simply and with no preamble as she sipped at the brew. She was thankful for that. Another man would have talked around the subject or suggested that this was not a task for her. Another would have insisted that they should carry the documents while she waited for them to return. Gothe did not make any such assumptions, or try to dissuade her, his only assumption that he would be going with her. That was one assumption for which she was thankful.

"Needs must," she replied with a certain resignation.

"They don't have to. You owe Mr West nothing," he said coldly.

"You're trying to talk me out of this?" she asked, surprised to say the least. "I would've thought you would want to encourage me to do this. We are after all trying to rescue your friend. Or is he just your employer?"

"He is both, and my charge," Gothe replied.

"Well then, as he is both your employer and your friend shouldn't you be telling me we need to do this?" she said, pulling her sleeve over the wrist strap to hide the second derringer like the first.

Gothe said nothing, which was more than a little infuriating. She looked him straight in his eyes, dark soulless pits that had none of the spark she should see there. It was the first time she had really noticed that. The utter absence of life in his eyes. In face of his silence she found herself wondering how it worked. The rational part of her mind dismissed the mystical hoodoo. He was not really dead. Corpses do not get up and walk around. Whatever had happened to Gothe, he was still alive even if he believed differently. That bottle he carried in his chest, well that could perhaps be explained. She was not sure how. His blood too, so thick, treacle like, that could probably be explained as well. Though again she was not sure how. An animated corpse given will, the idea was ridiculous to her rational mind. Yet here he was, and the irrational side of her was starting to half believe it was true…

She made herself break contact with that blank lifeless stare, no longer able to hold his gaze, and so she looked at the floor.

"We are doing this, Mr Gothe, dangerous or not. I will not leave Mr West or Constable Riley to Harrington's mercy," she said at last, surprising herself with the determination in her voice.

"Very good, Miss," he said, his face taking on a fair facsimile of a smile.

She nodded, and drank the last of the tea, before putting the journal and map into a canvas bag and making for the door.

She had made the doorway when he coughed loudly.

"Yes?" she inquired.

"Just one thing, Miss," he said.

"What is it, Gothe?" she questioned with just a hint of tiredness creeping into her tone.

"Well, Miss, would your father have had a gun of some kind around here?"

At this, she smiled. She walked towards the back of the office and a small compartment that had gone unnoticed in the desecration. "You know, Mr Gothe," she had told him. "I think I have just the thing."

And so, they were now standing there, on Sheers Wharf as the sun was going down, tucked into the recesses of a set of warehouse doors on the edge of the dock side.

Waiting.

They did not have long to wait.

Chapter Ten

The Battle of Sheers Wharf

As the last lazy rays of the sun sank below the roof tops, from the other side of the small yard a group of men entered. Five of whom she recognised. Harrington, of course, and his two favourite goons. The other two men she recognised were walking with wrists tied behind their backs. Even in the twilight it was easy to make out their faces, though poor Constable Riley was only just recognisable, the right side of his face a swollen blackened mess from the beating he had taken. Benjamin West had fared little better, one blackened eye and dried blood on his forehead. He was also favouring his left leg as he walked. Eliza was no expert, but it looked to her as if he was nursing a couple of fractured ribs. Either he had fought his capturers or else they had maliciously taken out their frustrations on him at the workshop.

There were four other men with the party, none of whom she recognised, but they looked like more hired thugs of the ilk of Mr's Instrument and Blunt, men either loyal to Harrington or to the pay day he had offered them. There was no doubting that these were men capable of violence to order. It also meant there were more of them than she had hoped. She thought of the two hidden derringers on spring-loaded mounts under her sleeves. Two shots apiece and at short range if you were looking to kill someone. *Best to hope it doesn't come to that*, she thought to herself. Though she was a little reassured because Mr Gothe standing beside her had hidden under his great coat something a tad more powerful than her own guns. That said she hoped they would just take the documents and let their prisoners go. It may have been a vain hope, but it was at least a hope.

Harrington and his thugs marched West and Riley out on to the Wharf. Twenty foot of desperate-looking walkway jutting out into the Thames. The wooden stilts it sat upon would be mired with green moss and rust where the iron nails had run with corrosion. At low tide there would have been a drop of twenty feet to mud flats below. Caked with the slurry and sewage dumped daily into the old father. All the filth and grime that was the underbelly of the industrial wonders of Victoria's golden age, and a city of a million souls whose waste had to go somewhere. The tide was high however, and at the swell of the waters lapped up the stilts and over the planking itself.

She watched as both captives were turned to face the landward side and forced down on to their knees. Rope was lashed around their ankles and tied to their wrists, leaving her in no doubt that they were helpless. Two of the thugs took up position behind them, while the rest walked back to the shore and stood waiting. The threat was all too apparent. Little more than a nudge would send either or both men into the river. They would have no hope once they were caught with in its watery grasp. Harrington had laid out his scene, saying loudly without words what would happen if he did not get his way.

Eliza, watched a while longer, letting a few minutes slip by. She was not sure why, perhaps hoping that it might set Harrington on edge when she did not show herself straight away. Let him wait a while and become nervous that he had misjudged her. It would be a small victory, petty even, to make him nervous, but it was better than nothing. Finally, as Harrington started to look more than a little irritated, she made to move out on to the gas lit dock side, only to be stopped by Gothe's hand on her shoulder.

"Wait, Miss, someone else has arrived," he whispered, pointing.

She followed her companion's finger and saw that a Hanson cab had just turned in to the yard, the driver seemingly oblivious to the scene before him, in the manner of cabbies everywhere. Late night fares to dark, half abandoned docksides tended to tip well and be none of your business. The size of the tip being the important matter.

"Who's in the cab?" she pondered half to herself.

Gothe did not venture an opinion, but she did not really expect him to speculate. She doubted he speculated a great deal about anything. She wondered if that was because of his condition or if he had always been like that. She was coming to suspect the latter may be the case. She rather hoped it was. Better his grim facade was merely indicative of his character, rather not a result of his less than alive condition.

Whoever was in the cab, their arrival seemed to irritate Harrington even more, an observation that brought a smile to her lips. It had already struck her that it was unlikely Harrington was doing all this for a map and a journal. He was no more than a petty gang boss with pretensions of grandeur as far as she knew. The new arrival was probably both his employer and the brains behind all that had occurred, and no one likes their boss watching them work. If it put Harrington a little further out of kilter, then that was all to the good. Besides which, she wanted to know who was behind the black cab's curtain. Whoever it was, she did not doubt they were as much to blame for her father's death as Harrington himself.

"Times wasting, Miss Maybe," Harrington, said loudly, clearly sick of waiting. "I'm sure you're here so you may as well show yourself before one of the young gentlemen behind me take a late-night swim."

She suspected the arrival of the cab had much to do with that. He was now determined to get a grip of the situation as he was in front of an audience.

A moment of doubt crept over her. If he was too on edge, it might be more dangerous. Whatever else he was, Harrington was normally rational. He was a businessman at the end of the day, even if it was a shady business that he engaged in. Now, however, he was stalking around like a scolded cat. She hesitated a moment longer, watching as Harrington turned and started back towards the pier. His short walk towards those he was willing to condemn was punctuated with words. "Very well, I think it's time to see how well the constable swims, don't you?"

"Wait," she heard herself shout, as she stepped out into the gas light, closely followed by her companion.

"Ah, Miss Maybe, makes her appearance at last, and the erstwhile Mr Gothe as well. I guess I shouldn't be surprised. I trust you've a package for me?" Harrington said, turning back to face them, a few feet from the prisoners. "I must admit I was starting to be more than a little concerned you were going to let the river have our friends here."

His tone was even, perhaps even playful. He no doubt sensed he had the upper hand in this encounter. She had to bite back her desire to tell him to go to hell, while fighting the itch at her wrists to shoot him on the spot. She feared the outcome would be nasty for all concerned if she did so however, and she had no wish to be responsible for the death of the two men bound on the wharf.

"You win, Harrington. Take the damn things," she said bitterly, throwing a satchel towards him that held the journal and map. "Now let those men free."

The skeletal Harrington walked slowly back towards her and retrieved the satchel. He took a moment to examine the contents then looked up at the cab by the main gates.

"A moment, Miss Maybe, if you don't mind. Just need to confirm these are indeed what we are after," he said, as if this was some normal business transaction, which it may well have been for him, she knew.

He made his way slowly to the cab, passing only a few feet from her in the process. She swallowed the bile that rose in her throat. That desire to shoot him was all the stronger with him so close. The desire to avenge her father with one swift movement. Snap up her arms and let both derringers bark out into the night. Harrington was not quite that foolish however. Four of his men still stood on the pier with his bargaining chips, while two others were even now taking up position to flank Eliza and Gothe. In their hands were heavy clubs, but she had no doubt they had firearms too about their persons. She had after all shot at their boss the day before. That alone would be enough to convince Harrington to make sure his men were armed with more than bits of wood.

He reached the cab and handed the satchel through the black curtained window. Words were exchanged, but too quietly for her to make out. Whatever was said, it seemed the occupant of the coach was satisfied. She heard the sound of a cane knocking on the cab's ceiling, and the cabbie pulled on the reins. The horses, quick to heed a command, set off into the rising mist and in moments the cab had pulled out of view. Harrington, leaning heavily on his cane, made his way back towards the wharf, a sly grin crossing his visage which bore no one good will, she was sure. Her palms itched again for the weight of her guns. A simple flick of the wrist to trigger the mechanism and they would rest in her hands… But she waited until he was passing in spitting distance before she spoke. Wanting him in close range, should he sour the deal.

"Okay, you've what you wanted, now set them free," she said, biting down her anger.

Harrington smiled, that nasty little smile of his. "Oh, but Miss Maybe, I don't believe I ever said I'd be letting them go free. Of course, if it were up to me, I'd be delighted to do so, but my employer in this enterprise… Well, he isn't a man for loose ends. It would all have been so much cleaner had your father just accepted my offer to buy them in the first place. It was a quite reasonable price, but he was a stubborn man, your father, I'd hoped that wasn't a family taint, but you proved intractable my dear… You should realise of course that you're now out of bargaining chips. You gave me what I wanted before getting what you want in return… Tut tut, my dear. You really should've brokered terms better, don't you think." He even went so far as to wag his finger at her when he said, 'Tut tut,' like a schoolmaster lecturing a student who had failed some simple arithmetic.

She almost shot him there and then. Instead, she raised her arms slowly, a move measured, not for him but for herself. She needed to stay in control, before things got out of hand. As it was, she let both derringers snap into her hands and pointed both at his odious face, the look that crossed it, a reward in of itself.

"I rather think you underestimate my bargaining skills, Mr Harrington," she said, aware in her peripheral vision that Gothe had moved to her side and pulled her father's gun out from beneath his long coat. That gave her much needed confidence. Her derringers were by nature small and looked less than threating, for all their ability to kill at close range. Her father's gun was however another matter. If any weapon was ever designed to look threatening then it was this one. Six high calibre barrels that shot in pairs, taking breach loads of heavy shot. A thing of steel and brass that was a mixture of shotgun and revolver. Gothe was taking pains to heft it and cover the other men. She did not turn to look but was aware that there was movement there too. No doubt they were raising weapons in kind. Harrington, she suspected, was trying regain his calm in the face of her guns, but the sweat on his brow told her he understood that he was well within the killing range of her two little pistols. She was silently daring him to make another remark about her father. Just one of his little witty comments. That would be all the excuse she would need, no matter how badly things went afterwards.

He managed that same sick little smile regardless. "I see I have indeed, Miss Maybe, but I should caution you against being too hasty. My men are all armed and your friends over there would find swimming even harder with bullets in them."

"You presume I wouldn't just be happy to put some brass in you and damn the consequences," she snapped out in reply, not entirely sure herself that she would not be. Oh, to put four bullets in him, both guns, both barrels, and just rely on Gothe to do for the rest of them. With their boss down, his men might just leg it, for all she knew. Besides what did she owe to either of the men on the dock anyway. Mr West was a rich man's son whose legacy had led to her father's death. As for Riley, well, coppers were less than useless down in Cheapside. He had only been stationed at her door because the police knocked it down in the first place. He had been in the wrong place at the wrong time... but he was hardly her responsibility. So here she was with the swine who did for her father in her sights once more, just like he had been at the funeral, and no one was going to step in the way of her shots this time. She could do for the bastard and be done with it...

"I'm sure a good young lady like yourself wouldn't want Mr West's death on your conscience." Harrington said, trying to appeal to her better nature, doubtless, voice as slick as the oil on the old river itself.

Eliza hesitated, and hated herself for it. Worse, Harrington could see her doing so and perhaps sensed weakness, like the sharks her father had told her of. Then he turned, slowly and quite deliberately showing his back to her and resumed his walk towards the pier.

"Cut the gentleman free," he said without pausing his stride, motioning towards Benjamin.

She gritted her teeth, wondering if Harrington knew how close he was to being shot in the back. Her trigger fingers itched, her arms felt like they were made of lead. She was suddenly terrified they would drop or loosen the triggers with no thought from her at all. And each stride took him closer to an invisible line on the flagstones that marked the limits of the effective range of her guns, and she let him keep walking…

She was better than him, had to be better than him, deep down she knew it. Had to know it… she had to let him walk away or she was just as bad as he was. A feeder shark dredging the bottom for the weak. She had to let West and Riley get clear. *Please god, let them get clear.* She had to, because if she shot Harrington in the back now, she was as bad as him.

Eliza watched as the henchmen cut the bonds holding Benjamin down as Harrington slipped beyond her range, at least that was unless she took a few steps forward, but she dared not risk it till the two men were free. Not now. The moment for belligerent rage had passed.

Free of his bonds, Benjamin stood stiffly and slowly walked back down the pier, a guard with a gun at his back. Eliza saw the stiffness of his gait once more. The nursed ribs, the dried blood on his forehead. As he passed the entrance to the pier itself and headed towards his rescuers, the guard fell back alongside the two who stood at the edge of the wharf. Harrington himself moved to stand to the side of them, then a step back, their bulk between him and her guns. She took her gaze off him and looked at the still prone constable Riley. A surge of sympathy overtook her. A young man in the wrong place at the wrong time. She remembered he had been quick with a smile and a bit of cheek. She suddenly knew for certain he did not deserve to be kneeling on that wharf with a bust open face and was horrified she had contemplated abandoning him to his fate only moments before.

"And the constable," she said with as much authority as she could muster.

Harrington however shook his head. "Really, Miss Maybe, that won't do. No one of any importance is going to take notice of you three. My employer I don't doubt will spread money about to make sure of that. But even the most corrupt of Peel's finest take umbrage with one of their own taking a beating. So, you must see the position that puts me in. It's better for us all really if the constable here goes for a late-night swim. Can't be relied upon to keep his mouth shut about the goings on of his betters. You can have your gentleman by all means, but this one has to disappear, I'm afraid…"

She wondered again who the occupant of the Hanson had been. *Someone with enough pull not to be worried what may be said*, she guessed… Well, that came as little surprise when it came to herself. Lady justice may be blind, but if you were an engineer's daughter form Cheapside, let alone one of mixed race, she was bloody deaf as well. But West… he was a gentleman of some sort, he had money, family, he would have connections. Harrington was not so stupid that he did not realise that. Yet he was still prepared to let him walk away. *Just who was in that carriage?*

"Let the constable go," she said again, taking a step forwards, a dangerous step it proved as the henchmen's guns all came up and pointed at her. But she was now close enough to see the fear in the constable's eyes. The injustice of his situation brought her rage back to the surface. Her fingers itched once more.

West was almost alongside her now and she noted an almost imperceivable nod between him and Gothe. A flicker of recognition that would be lost on the thugs at his back but enough to tell Gothe and Eliza he was ready. Ready for what she had no idea, but he was ready all the same.

"Very well," Harrington said, and turned with a step so he was behind the bulk of Mr Blunt. "Mr Instrument, if you would be so kind as to let the constable go." He instructed his henchman but his words were belied by his hand gesturing across his throat. A gesture that even the most dim-witted of goons knows.

"No…" she heard herself saying.

"Goodbye, Miss Maybe," Harrington added, almost as an afterthought.

Then everything happened at once.

The thug on the wharf struck his victim from behind with a billy club, sending him sprawling into the river. Harrington turned and headed towards the warehouse he had emerged from, keeping himself behind the human barrier of Mr Blunt.

Two of the other thugs' pistols sang out, and Gothe returned in kind with two of his six barrels, the noise of which was deafening. His marksmanship was better than the thugs, who shot wide. The first of the thugs pitched backwards as Gothe's shots took him in the chest. The second brute's shooting took off Mr Gothe's hat and Eliza felt a sting cross her arm as a bullet grazed past. Her own guns went off, at the limits of effective range, one taking

Blunt high in the leg, but not enough to even slow him. The second bullet must have gone wide completely.

Gothe threw the gun to West and was suddenly running for the river. Somehow, she found the time to wonder at this seemingly vain act. Riley had already sunk without a trace; in the dim light she could not even see ripples to mark his passing. Even as she wondered at it all, she was moving forwards, re-cocking the derringers for the second shot each held.

One thug was helping the downed one to his feet, firing blindly, more in hope than judgement. Harrington was almost free and clear at the warehouse door and Mr Blunt was turning to face her, a face enraged by the pain she had doubtless inflicted.

Benjamin swung the gun around. By luck alone he must have figured out how to rotate the barrels and re-cock the gun but doing so had slowed him a little.

Gothe went into the river at a run, the surge of water crashing across Mr Instrument as he made for the shore. This was enough to mess with his aim and send his own shots wide of West.

Eliza shot at Harrington, ignoring Mr Blunt completely and was rewarded with a cry of pain from the odious little man as he fell through the doorway. But she had no time to savour the victory or the feeling of triumph that flashed over her, not knowing if she had winged him or struck a real blow, as Mr Blunt crashed into her and she was sent flying to the ground.

More gun fire, the eruption of her father's gun, and a heavy splash as something or someone went into the river.

Her head suddenly felt light, odd, her vision blurring and something damp ran down her neck as she lay under the weight of Mr Blunt. She could see him struggling to raise a gun and point it directly at her face while he was still pinning her down with his weight. His face was all twisted with rage and murderous intent. There was shouting and another blast of her father's gun.

Her name… Someone shouted her name…

Was it her father…? No, the voice was all wrong.

But who would be using her father's gun but her father? Where was she?

The world became darker still…

She heard the barking thunder of another gun.

Then there was nothing.

Chapter Eleven

Perturbing
Awakenings

She was six years old, sitting by the fire, eyes closed, imagining the heat from the flames was the sun on her face, as he told her of the islands. This strange man, skin darker than hers, with eyes that smiled. Telling her of this far off land where the sea was blue, and waves rolled over beaches of white sand. Where the sun was warm even in winter. Where trees grew nuts the size of your head and covered in hair. Where the people were all painted, like he was painted, with swirling concentric patterns on his face surrounding those smiling eyes. Her told her of the trade wind that blew across the shore. Of birds with feathers all the colours of the rainbow that could learn your words and speak them back you...

"This is your father," her mother had told her. This painted man with skin so dark it made hers seem pale. This man of smiles and such wondrous tales of the far-off islands in the sun.

She was eight, standing in the rain. A world that was grey, as grey as the stones in their badly made rows. A hole in the ground. A box lowered. Tears lost in the rain. Her mother gone. No more her rasping coughs in the night. A large hand held hers, dark skin, rough, calloused.

"She's at peace now, on the next island," lied a voice that brought comfort it could barely spare for the need of its own. A voice telling her of his people, her people, of the great cycle, of the island to come.

Pretty lies... Lies told for the telling when the truth would hurt even more. Pretty lies told by eyes surrounded by the spirals, and a smile full of sorrow for what went in the ground.

She was twelve and watching iron and brass, moulded by hands darker than her own. Telling of wonders of metal and gears. Telling of steam and cylinders, strange words given meaning... Flux and pressure… Compressor and valve… Strange words spoken with all the wonder of islands in the sun. She was learning, with knowledge, given of love.

She was fourteen and told she should dream. So, she surprised him with spirals all of her own. The first had said no when she said what she wanted. But the third had agreed and she came home to him painted as was he.

His face grew angry, at what she had done, but by morning he had forgiven her and sang her a song. A song of the islands. A song for a woman grown.

Then he showed her new wonders, designs of his own.

She was nineteen. Stood over him. Watching over him.

The smiling eyes were dull now.

The skin darker than her own was burning.

Sickly he whispered confused words, while she spoke of the islands to him, trying to remember his own words.

Then…

The graveside.

The heaviness of grief…

No more smiling eyes…

Eliza woke, and knew at once she was not anywhere she should be. The memory of the dream was fading already as only dreams faded. The mixed emotions it had stirred were replaced with an anxious awareness that she was not in her own bed, or any bed she would be accustomed to. It was the sheets that felt wrong to her, soft, white linen. She had never slept in white linen in her life. She was used to heavy practical blankets of coarse wool. Clean blankets always, she made sure of that, but never linen. She instinctively felt she should not be there. Not in a place of white linen. There was no white linen anywhere she should be…

She took stock of her surroundings; she was in a light and airy room. Curtains were pulled open to reveal a large sash window. The walls were a bright white colour and hung with paintings in soft pastels. It was a room, she felt, too large for sleeping in. The bed itself was too large. A couple's bed, not the narrow single cot she was used to. There was too much space, too much light and way too much clean. Not that her own room back at the workshop was ever anything but clean, but this was a different type of clean. This was a clean that had never known dirt to start with.

It was then she realised something else, something even more profoundly wrong. She was dressed in a heavy cotton nightgown. A nightgown that was not her own.

Her head felt wrong. She felt muggy, clouded of thought. She raised a hand to it and felt a lump and a line of rough skin, a scab still healing. Her left arm throbbed slightly and as she examined herself, she found another healing wound. It was then she remembered the bullet that grazed a hot line across it, and the memory of the fight at Sheers Wharf came flooding back to her.

The gun fire. The shouting. The smell of gun smoke and the stink of the river.

She remembered the face of the man holding her down. Mr Instrument, or Blunt, she could not remember which. She remembered the stink of his sweat though and the snarling twisted face so full of rage as he tried to raise his gun to her head.

She started shaking, the memory overwhelming her, and the shock of waking in a strange room. Her wrist felt naked without her derringers, and she wanted them suddenly. Wanted something, anything solid of her own. Her clothes would be a start. To be somewhere she knew would be better, but right at the moment, the memories of Sheers Wharf so sharp in her mind, her guns would be best of all.

She heard the door creaking and she sat up sharply. She felt an urge to bolt. To confront whoever was about to enter this strange place she had found herself in. Wild thoughts rampaged through her mind. Had she been captured? Was she in some kind of hospital? Was she a prisoner? Was this all some trick of Harrington's?

Harrington… She had shot him. Actually shot him. She had wanted to. She had been almost desperate to. But she never actually imagined she would… But she had not killed him, she was sure of that. Was he the one coming through the door…?

She set herself, ready to leap at the intruder. She grabbed the only thing to hand, a small vase by the side of the bed, and hefted it ready to use.

Come on then, you bastard, come in and see what you're get…'

"Good morning, Miss. Glad you're awake at last. We were beginning to worry about you, I don't mind telling you," said the woman in the maid's uniform as she walked in holding a sliver tray. A silver tray with a tea service laid out upon it. A silver tray that also contained a silver toast rack complete with toasted bread.

Eliza realised suddenly how hungry she was…

The maid was in her middle years, perhaps her late thirties. Her grey streaked hair was tied up in a bun and fighting for freedom against it, her uniform neatly pressed. She looked exactly what Eliza would have expected a domestic maid to look like… Yet still she was on edge. None of this was right.

"Third time I've brought this tray up this morning, and four times yesterday. The gentleman said not to disturb you. 'Doctor's orders,' he said. Though I think Doctor Lindsey is just an old fuss pot and no mistake. I said to him, 'When she wakes up, she'll want to have a nice cup of tea and a bit of grub,' I said. Best medicine in the world that is…"

The way the maid talked was like a waterfall of words. Tumbling out of her and running over themselves to be said. Each as desperate as the last to be out before the previous one was fully spoken

"Anyway, the gentleman said what with you being sad-ate-ide by Doc Lindsey and all, you could sleep for another day yet. But I said to myself, Alice, she's going to wake up at some point so just you keep checking. Cause she's gon'na need a cheery face when she does and a nice cuppa after everything she been through. Oh, and that was a right palaver that was an' no mistake. His nibs goes disappears off for a few days then turns up at gone five in the morning, shouting an carrying on. Then he sends my poor Sam for old Lindsey, and him having barely woken up. Then Mr Gothe, oh, he was in such a state, carries you up 'ere and dumps you on the bed, big lunk. Why it weren't decent, I said to him. I said, 'Mr Gothe, the poor lass needs putting to bed proper and not with the likes of you in the room,' I said. Chased him out I did and got you decent like for when the doctor arrived. Well, the doctor was in a right strop being called out at all hours, but the gentleman was having none of it and insisted like, 'She's to have the best care,' he said. Oh he was in a foul mood, and bleeding all over the rug he was but you had to be seen to first, he said. Oh, he tore poor old Doc Lindsey a right strip he did. Then this 'In-spec-tor' turns up and starts braying on the door and my Sam had Butle' for his nibs while they were up there in the drawing room, calling for a fresh pot. Didn't wipe his boots or nothing and that floor fresh scrubbed."

Somehow in-between the endless stream of words, the maid had placed the tray on a small table by the side of the bed, poured the tea and was halfway back out the door without Eliza getting a word in edgeways.

"I'll tell his lordship you're awake. I'm sure he'll be pleased, been worried sick, so he has, and Mr Gothe, I'm sure, not that he ain't said a word but I know he was worried too. Never says much that one, oh, grim as death he is sometimes. He didn't wipe his boots neither and he should know better. Had half a mind to tell him to scrub the floor himself. State he was in, it was like he'd bin walking through the river. Stank to high heaven as well, had to scrub that greatcoat of his clean I did and then he..."

And with that, the door closed and she was gone, though the maid's voice lingered as she walked away, muffled by the door. Clearly, she was still talking away to herself even though her audience had been left alone in the room behind her.

"Well, that answers some questions," Eliza muttered to herself.

She was still feeling a little lightheaded, like the world was myopic, all blurred edges and fuzzy lines. She drank the tea with slow sips, letting the warm liquid revive her as she tried to shake off the haze. The torrent of one-sided conversation from Alice at least provided her with some knowledge of where she was, though she knew little of the why. She had been injured in the gunfight, that much was obvious, even without her recollections of everything going to hell at Sheers Wharf. But obviously she had not been injured too badly. The wound on her arm was throbbing, as was her head, but beyond that and general fuzziness, which she could put down to having been sedated, she felt fine.

As she put the jigsaw of the maid's words and her surroundings together, she realised she must be at the abode of Benjamin West, which meant she was in Kensington, if she remembered rightly, or somewhere close to there. But none of this answered the most important question her present circumstances presented to her. That being, where her clothes were?

She finished the tea and snaffled down the toast. Then got out of bed and started to explore the room. A wardrobe off to one side proved to be empty but for an old pair of men's boots that looked too small for any man's feet. A child's she assumed, and long forgotten by the look of them. At the foot of the bed she found a travelling trunk, a heavy wooden thing. She pondered for a moment before opening it. It was, after all, not the done thing to go rooting through other people's belongings. She rationalised, however, that it was also not the done thing to leave a woman without her clothes, in a short nightdress, in a strange bedroom. So she opened the lid of the trunk after struggling slightly with straps fashioned by someone who was determined they would not break open by accident, or indeed on purpose if you did not want to strain yourself doing so. She was somewhat relieved, if slightly perturbed, to find it contained her clothes from the night at the wharf. Cleaned and pressed by someone, presumably the chatterbox Alice. She was further perturbed that it also contained most of her wardrobe from back at the workshop.

She felt a cold flash of rage. Someone had been through her things. Worse, they had collected them all and had shipped them here. Wherever here was. She was, she determined, going to have words with Mr Benjamin West. They would, she decided, be choice words, some of them not the kind of words that a young lady like she should probably know or let alone say. But that flash of anger aside, she was, she admitted to herself, glad her clothes were there and so she set about pulling them out, and felt a moment of genuine delight to find that her spring mounted wrist straps, along with the derringers were also in the trunk, buried under the neatly pressed clothes.

She leaned into the trunk to pull them out.

It was she later reflected typical that at this point she heard the door to the room open once more. Just as she was leaning deep into the recesses of the trunk, in a borrowed nightdress.

To Eliza's utter embarrassment, she heard Benjamin West's voice stammer, "Oh my… I do apologise… I didn't… I mean I knew you were up… but I didn't think you would be up… up… not expect you to be out of bed… I… erm …"

A minor ice age seemed to pass for Eliza, which was probably no more than a few seconds. The time it took for Mr West to realise he was standing in a doorway, staring at a woman he barely knew, who was bent over a large wooden trunk, in a night dress.

Meanwhile Eliza was suddenly acutely aware of the short nature of the nightdress, which presumably had been borrowed for her comfort from Alice the maid, a woman a good six inches shorter than Eliza.

"Oh… I… That is…" he started saying, then presumably realised that what a gentleman should do in this situation, aside not be in this situation in the first instances, was to bid a hasty retreat.

The door slammed shut once more. Though it had not shut fast enough for Eliza's liking. Her inner rage was all the rawer for it, fast becoming a well of resentment, deep and dark. She wanted to slam something heavy. To scream at West, claw at him, show him exactly how angry she was. Bursting into her room, catching her wearing nothing but that ridiculous nightdress, and sprawled over a trunk. *God, does the man not even have the sense to knock? Doesn't even bloody leave straight away, he stands there gawping and stammering his bloody apologies. Well, he can stuff his damn apologies…* her anger raged.

Then as she calmed down a little, she remembered how shocked he had sounded, how unsure he had been about what to say or do. Like a rabbit caught in a lamper's light. She thought about Mr West, always trying to be so calm, so assured, so easy with a smile and a jest, yet it seemed, so easily befuddled. He was like a child. A child caught doing something they should not be doing. Paralysed, and helpless in a situation beyond their control, with no idea how to extricate himself.

She had not seen the expression on his face at the time, what with being head down in the trunk. Yet she could picture it quite clearly…

Eliza started to chuckle, and then laugh, all the tension that had built up in her evaporating with the laughter. She laughed long and loud, then found herself wondering if he was still standing outside her door, plucking up the courage to knock upon it. Out there hearing her laughter.

A thought that only made her laugh all the harder.

Chapter twelve

You should've shot him

An hour later, Eliza was shown into the library by the stream of vocalised conscious thought as she had come to think of Alice, the maid, who it seemed had just picked up her earlier one-sided conversation where she had left off the moment she reappeared at Eliza's door. The constant chatter was grating on Eliza's nerves. It was not so much that she minded the constant deluge of mostly nonsensical diatribes, it was more, she reflected as they made had their way down a wide staircase, that it would have been nice to get a word in edgeways.

Despite this minor irritation, there was at least a certain freeness of information flowing from the vocal cords of the maid. If you could find a way to direct the conversation to subjects you wanted to know about then you could have learned anything you desired. But as directing the conversation seemed impossible, Eliza found herself just listening with half an ear in the vain hope that she could pick up something important.

The walk from her room to the library had taken them along a short corridor and down a grand staircase, then through a couple of doors and up another staircase of dark oak. All along the route the walls were lined with paintings of intermittent quality. A mix of grand landscapes and austere portraits. They and the décor gave the house a feeling of money, old dusty money. Money that had been harvested and hoarded over many generations. Some of the paintings were doubtless of old patriarchs of the family. Some of which had a stark similarity to Benjamin West. The same cheekbones and firm brow passed on down the family line. Eliza had been vaguely aware he was a gentleman of independent means. What she had not considered was the extent of those means. This was old money extensive. Family pile in the Cotswolds and an inheritable seat in the house extensive.

Alice was a less than informing guide when it came to family history, however. Her main concerns seemed to be the need to scrub floors because of muddy boots and irritation at having to make pots of tea for callers at strange hours. There was someone called 'My Sam' who might be her husband, or her son, or just the other household servant over whom she felt a degree of ownership. Sam, according to Alice, was much put upon, though the extent of his being put upon seemed to revolve around him having to do things that left Alice sweeping the floors and doing the polishing herself.

Up the second staircase which Eliza was sure was longer than the first, they reached another landing which led to the library. The house, it seemed to her, was wrong, or at least its internal dimensions struck her as wrong, until she realised it was actually two houses adjoined. At some point in the past, the West family abode had extended into a neighbouring house. Which was just more proof of old family money. To say houses in Kensington did not come cheap was an understatement akin to London's smog was misty.

Finally, as they reached the door to what Alice informed her was the 'Master's Library', and the stream of vocal rainfall abruptly ceased. Alice paused for a second to straighten her uniform, then knocked on the old oak door with a servant's politeness. Then without waiting for permission from the occupant she opened the door carefully.

"Your guest, My Lord," the maid said with a certain stiffness of tone and reverence which spoke of the deference to social positions.

The change of Alice's tone of voice, as much as anything else, alerted Eliza to an odd realisation. Alice had clearly been talking to her as an equal. As a part of the below stairs tier of the household. Not that this realisation took her greatly by surprise. Though she had not thought in those terms earlier. But of course, Mr West was the master of the house, and was therefore held at a certain distance by those below stairs. Despite her being a guest in the household, Eliza was still a working-class girl from Cheapside. Her clothes may not have been rags but they did not speak of money either. Her accent was a mix of the east end and a smattering of her father's Polynesian tones she had gained by osmosis, which also marked her as belonging downstairs. And then of course there was the colour of her skin, while not as dark as her father's had been, a white English mother and an islander father had gifted her with the dark olive skin of southern Italy or Spain, and that was certainly a downstairs skin tone in the houses of the English gentry.

While she doubted Alice knew she was thinking in such terms, she had demarked Eliza's social position and seen an equal to whom she could talk openly. A fellow scrubber of floors who for the moment was residing in the upper house but was sure to be doing so briefly. Had it been otherwise then it would have been a different Alice the maid that Eliza had met that morning. One who would have been treated her as deferentially as she was now treating the master of the house.

Eliza found it difficult not to resent such an assessment, but she also found it difficult to disagree with. She was thankful that Alice seemed not be bear her any resentment for residing above her station, which would hardly have been a surprise had she done so, and decided she liked the woman. She would just have liked her better if she let a conversation flow in more than one direction…

In the library, when she was ushered in by Alice, Eliza found Benjamin huddled over a desk at the far end of the room. He seemed intent in a study of some loose bits of paper and several books laying open in a scatter of disorganised piles. The room itself was not as large as Eliza expected. Little bigger than the bedroom she had awoken in. The walls were however lined with bookshelves and display cabinets that held strange-looking items of antiquity, or ethnic origin. A tribal shield and spearhead that belonged to some African tribe. Jars containing pickled samples of oddities. A couple of stone statues that seemed to depict things which were not quite human and were probably sacred relics of some distant culture or other. A pair of Chinese vases with jade dragons painted around them. There was even, much to Eliza's distaste, what appeared to be the shrunken head of some unfortunate with hair still attached and a disproportionate grin. It was a collection of imperial acquisition. The detritus of the world swept up unceremoniously into an Englishman's study.

She stood in the doorway a moment, watching West absorbed in his studies. Even though she had been announced, he seemed unaware of her presence until he absently looked up, and a flicker of alarm crossed his face. "Oh, Eliza, very good, come in please. Alice… Erm… Tea, if you please," he said before immediately returning to the page he was studying.

There was a briskness about him that did not quite stack with the man Eliza had met a few days before. His mannerisms and character were different here. In this house he was master of his domain. Whatever deference he exhibited in the world beyond evaporated. Here he was used to just doing as he would and the world fitting around him. Perhaps that was why he barged into her room without knocking… He clearly owned the place, in more ways than one.

"My lord," Alice replied stiffly and retreated from the room, closing the door behind her, leaving Eliza alone in Benjamin's company, feeling awkward and unsure of herself. Her residual anger at waking in a strange bed, in a strange house, still smouldered. Though the knowledge of her injuries and the need for a doctor, lessened her anger a little. Still she wondered why she had been brought here and not taken back to the workshop. Was she like the objects in the cabinets of this room, she wondered, an oddity to a wealthy man, an acquisition brought to the house on the master's whim? That was an idea she found disturbing, but once it occurred to her she could not quite shake it. What did Benjamin West want of her? And why was he leaving her just standing in the room while he read. Well, of course, she was just a working-class girl, and he the lord of the manor… *I'm expected to wait on his pleasure, well we will see about that*, she thought, her rage far from depleted.

He looked up, after another minute or so, from the papers once more and waved her over. "Eliza, it's good to see you up and about at last," he said, as if that smoothed things over.

"You saw rather more of me than you should have done an hour ago," she snapped back at him with belligerent sharpness. She was determined to get some control over the situation she found herself in. He might be 'My Lord' in this house but she was damned if she was going to let him play that part with her. He most definitely was not her lord.

"Yes, I apologise once more for my intrusion," he said with genuine embarrassment in his voice, flushing slightly.

Then added, almost as an afterthought, "I didn't expect you to be out of bed."

She gave him a withering look that would have belied any acceptance of his apology. "You should learn to knock on doors…" she half muttered in reply.

He managed to look sheepish at this. Enough so that she almost forgave him. She guessed he was unused to knocking on doors in his own house. With the slightest of 'harrumph's' she let it slide and walked over to join him at the desk, taking a moment to look closer at the scattering of papers. She quickly recognised it as the incomplete copy of the journal Fredricks had done for her hastily, before she left for Sheers Wharf with the original. Gothe no doubt had informed West of its existence and West had arranged for its collection from the workshop. She had been in no state to do so after the events at the wharf.

The wharf… it felt like that had all happened the day before, but she had no idea how long she had been lying sedated in the room she had awoken in. Questions sprang to mind. Questions she vocalised without realising the anger and urgency in her tone. "What happened at the wharf? What have I missed? Why did you bring me here?"

"I thought it for the best," he said in reply to the last question, then let out a deep sigh. Trying, she suspected, to buy a moment before he launched into his explanation. She had a feeling he had one rehearsed and all her resentment welled up at once.

"I don't give a fig for what you thought was best, Mr West," she snapped at him and was rewarded by a pained expression crossing his face.

His expression was enough for her to realise she was being belligerent. She took a deep breath of her own, letting a little calm settle upon her, reminding herself that even if his reasons for bringing her to his home were flawed, she had been unconscious at the time. She did not doubt that leaving her at the wharf was never an option. Not quite meeting his gaze, she said with more measured tones, "I'm sorry, Mr West, I'm sure you had reasons, I would however like to hear them."

He smiled weakly and nodded his understanding. "How much do you remember?" he asked.

"Not much after the shooting started," she admitted. Then, as she remembered the sound of a body going into the water, she asked with a certain amount of dread in her tone. "Constable Riley?"

"Alive, thank god, well, thank Gothe. He got him out before he drowned. Luckily, he was unconscious when he went in, which probably stopped him swallowing too much of the filth in the river. We brought him back here too, but he left with Inspector Grace yesterday."

"Grace has been here?"

"Even in Cheapside, gunfire and corpses draw attention," he said with a genuine smile. "I sent word to him once we had you safely back here and spoke with him yesterday. I suspect he will be back some time this evening to check on things."

She fell silent for a moment, trying to process. She was not sure she wanted more involvement with the police. They were never particularly welcome in the streets of Cheapside. They tended to bring their own problems with them. West was wrong to assume that corpses and gunfire in Cheapside would have drawn the attention of the authorities, but it did not seem worth dissuading him of that belief now. Having said that, things were getting out of hand. There were also still too many of her questions still unanswered. The chief of those occurred to her now. "Harrington?"

West's smile faded. "Got away, unfortunately."

"So, he is still out there."

"Unfortunately… I think you winged him if it's any consolation. I'm fairly sure he took one of your little bullets to the leg just before his thug jumped you," he said, grinning.

"Blunt?" she asked, ignoring the 'little bullets' quip.

"If that was his name, yes."

"Was?"

"He had you pinned to the ground and was trying to shoot you. I'd a choice between him or Harrington. So I shot him before he shot you."

"You should have shot Harrington," she said with a certain vehemence.

"I think not," West replied calmly. "As it was, I barely shot Mr Blunt in time. His gun went off as he fell and left you with that graze on your head. Otherwise, I fear it would have been the end of you, my dear Miss Tu-Pa-Ka. We would've all been most put out if that had happened."

"I don't care. You should've shot Harrington," she snapped, angry again. Irrationally so and she knew it. She fought for calm again, took a breath and tried to change her tone. "I'm sorry. It appears I owe you my life, Mr West. I thank you for that," she managed with some grace.

His smile returned, a genuine affection in his face she had not expected to see, or perhaps had been unable to see with anger clouding her judgement.

"My dear Eliza, I wouldn't have been there to save your life had you not come to my rescue in the first place. So on that score I believe I owe you far more than you owe me."

"You're being ridiculous," she replied, suddenly feeling flushed, a wave of embarrassment washing over her. She was not comfortable with praise. Least of all from the likes of Benjamin West.

"I think not. Harrington would happily have disposed of me, I'm sure. The man has a vile streak of petty vendetta about him, and I'd been a fly in the ointment so to speak."

He sighed heavily, as if anticipating an argument over what he was about to say next. "Which is also why I brought you here. While Harrington's loose, he's more than capable of wreaking a little malice in the world and upon you in particular. I want you safe, Miss Tu-Pa-Ka, and Cheapside is, I fear, far from safe for you right now."

"I can handle myself, Mr West," she said, fuming slightly at the suggestion. "Cheapside is my home. I'm sure I know it far better than a moneyed gentleman like yourself."

"Oh, I have no doubt of that, but it's beside the point. You were injured and even if you were not, your father's workshop is clearly far from safe right now. If nothing else, the events of the last few days have shown us this. If Harrington comes for you there…"

"Then he will regret it dearly because I'll not miss again," she interrupted, the edge to her voice giving him no doubt as to her feelings on the matter, to judge by the look on his face. But she went on anyway… "I'm not some helpless little girl, Mr West."

West started to laugh. She was about to be offended once more when he held up a hand in a gesture of surrender. "No, Miss Tu-Pa-Ka, you are as far from helpless as it is possible to be, I suspect."

She relaxed once more.

He took a deep breath and a moment's pause before he continued. When he did, his tone was serious once more. "You were, as I say, unconscious at the time. If you wish to return to the workshop, I will certainly not detain you. I seriously doubt I could if I tried. But I would prefer you to stay for a while, at least until hopefully that odious swine Harrington's in irons. Inspector Grace is rather adamant about that coming to pass. It seems that the police take unkindly to one of their own being kidnapped and less still when someone tries to kill them."

"I'm surprised even that moves them to do a great deal," she replied more bitterly than she intended. If the police were running Harrington down, it was a good thing, she admitted to herself. But she would be surprised if they actually found him. A rat like Harrington could disappear for months and resurface once the chase had gone cold. Men like Harrington were too canny to get caught.

"There's another reason I would ask you to stay," West said, she suspected to change the subject.

"Oh. And what is that?"

"Well, these actually," he said, gesturing at the copies of the journal that littered his desk. "I'm not sure I understand fully what they're referring to, but my father left me a letter directing me to yours. In that, he stated these papers were important. These and the map your father held. Whatever they are about, your father was killed for them, and I'd rather like to know why. More importantly, I'd like to know who was behind it."

"The Hanson at the wharf…"

"Exactly. Harrington's a nasty piece of work, but that's all he is. Someone else wanted the map and papers. Someone with power enough to orchestrate all this and who knows more about them than we do. Someone who unfortunately has the originals and the map, which judging by what I've read is the most important part of this whole thing…" He stopped, l ooking straight at her. He must have seen the smile that was crossing her lips. "What?" he inquired

"I doctored the map. They may have it but it's incomplete," she told him, unable to stop herself from smiling.

"You doctored it?"

"I cut off the bottom third. It's as good as useless to them and there is a chance, they'll not even realise."

West laughed, a deep hearty laugh, his own grin matching hers.

"You ceaselessly amaze me, Miss Maybe… Sorry, Miss Tu-Pa-Ka… It's just a shame you didn't get a copy of the map done while you got the journal copied."

Eliza smiled at him, thinking of the tattoo that covered her back. Painful as it was when she moved, it was hard to forget. "Oh. I've a copy, Mr West… So perhaps you should tell me what it is I have a copy of?"

The look of surprise and incredulity that crossed his face broadened her smile all the more. He was clearly unaware of her tattoo. Which was a surprise as she had suspected Gothe would have told him about her late-night visit to Fredricks. Perhaps she had underestimated Gothe's position in all this. Perhaps he really was looking out for her best interests after all. Well, if so, that was to the good. She had a secret to grasp hold of, something that gave her leverage… except, someone had stripped her. Put her in nightclothes. Alice the maid, she had to give Benjamin that much credit, he was too much the gentleman to stay while a female servant got her stripped and dressed in night clothes.

She thought about Alice and the chances of her secret tattoo staying secret for long. The woman who held it talked with the rapidity of a weaver's shuttle… She could hardly be expected to hold her silence on anything… But no, that was backstairs talk. Whatever the servants might know there was no reason the master would be told… If they saw her as 'backstairs' like them, they may well say nothing of it to anyone. She could only hope on that score.

The map was the heart of the mystery after all. That strange old Spanish map she suspected dated from the era of the conquistadors. Her own geography was patchy to say the least. Born and raised in Cheapside she was only dimly aware of the layout of the rest of her own city. But she was sure it had been a map of some part of South America.

She regretted the way she had kept a copy. A tattoo was a damn fool idea. But she had a copy, that was the important thing right now. Sure the words written upon it were ones she did not understand, and given where the copy lay, it was hard for her to read them now. But that was beside the point, the map was leverage, valuable, and whatever it was of lay at the heart of everything. Being in possession of the only complete copy, indeed being the only complete copy, gave her a position of power in all this. She had lost her father over that map and her life in many respects. If the damn thing was of value, she was going to make damn sure she got her share.

West, who had she suspected been wondering how much he should tell her, was looking at her thoughtfully. Then his eyes darkened as he seemed to reach a decision.

"Well, if these notes are correct, and as it's in my father's hand, I'm inclined to give them some credence. He clearly believed it to be the case at any rate. Well, the thing is, according to these notes it's… " he explained stutteringly, still sounding unsure, though it seemed what he was most unsure of was what reaction she would have to what he was trying, and failing, to tell her.

"For god's sake, Mr West, will you come out with it. My father's dead because of all this. I've been shot. My home's been burglarised. Bloody gunfights in Cheapside, Mr West. Gunfights I have been in the middle of… I think I have a right to know why, so out with it, damn you," she berated.

"Okay. Well, it seems…" he stumbled.

"Just tell me…" she snapped, mildly exasperated with his dithering, and he met her gaze, looking apologetic.

"Well… it seems the map shows the location of the fountain of youth," he said, every inflection in his voice suggesting he was utterly serious.

She said nothing… just stared at him.

"You see, well these papers say… Well, you see…"

"Read them to me!" she snapped, with an edge to her voice that West was clearly not entirely comfortable with.

Chapter Thirteen

A West Went West

January 2nd

The weather remarkable in its clemency. We left London and headed to the channel. Maybe left at dawn having completed final checks on the new engines and condenser. I wished him well in his new venture and hope it is not the last I see of London, Maybe and my boy Benjamin. He had grown once more this visit home, yet I wonder how much he will have grown when I see him next. Perhaps he will be a man. Oh that my Jane could have seen him grow to manhood. I fear she would not forgive me leaving him once more. But he is too young for this journey and a boy needs schooling. Beside he has her eyes, and the pain of her loss is too keenly felt when I look at the boy. It is better for him and me that we be apart. Perhaps when he is older, when her loss is not so sharp in my heart, I will be able to face the child our love begat upon the world. I cannot become maudlin on such matters; the boy deserves a father's love and that I would not deny him.

Such matters aside, the crew are in good spirits as we steam towards the channel and the first leg of our journey. Even those few who were with me at Millers Court have, like me, put those events behind us. Farnsworth will have to stew in his own juices until I return.

Jan 15th

Fogbound in the mid-Atlantic. A curse on Joles Collain. Waited three days in Cherbourg for him to arrive from Paris. Then two more days until his baggage arrived. For a tuppence I would have left him behind but for the need of his cartography. Delayed further by a late winter storm, it was the better side of a week before we were underway once more. Rough seas and fog caused us to sail at half steam. Thoughts of home are behind me now at least. I have little time for such matters now I can focus on the journey and a hundred tasks that require my attention. Have begun a full inventory after discovering not all the equipment I ordered was delivered. We will have to resupply when we make port in Havana.

Jan 16th

Still fog bound. Lost a crewman in the night. Drunk from the rum barrel, he fell from the port side. Ill luck it seems abounds us so early in this voyage. First missing supplies, now this. Some of the crew hold to old seamen's suspicions even in this enlightened age. Those that knew of Millers Court have been speaking of it despite my cautioning them not to. This fog saps the cheer from us all and Collain has been complaining of the lack of amenities aboard ship. Damn fool, did he expect a pleasure cruise? Lord save me from Frenchmen.

Jan 17th

The fog finally lifted and under full steam at last. Had to caution Edward Gothe for drinking, man was always a drunk ashore, but I have never known him in his cups at sea before. Had him locked in the brig to sober up. If he persists, may have to relieve him of his post when we make Cuba. Would be a sad day to lose him, he has been on my crewman these last ten years, since the islands and before. It seems without Maybe's steadying influence he reverts back to the thuggery I thought he had left behind.

Still we make good progress and we are making up some of the time we lost.

Jan 14th

Storm brewing to the south. We turned north for half the day to outrun it. Maybe's condensers are a wonder, running full steam on half the coal. I must write to him in Havana to commend his inventions once more.

Jan 15th

Gothe was drunk again and started fighting with Jeffreys over dice. Have locked them both in brig to cool off. I am losing patience with the man.

Jan 19th

Clear skies, and the Caribbean. Jeffreys back on duty. Gothe however moans in the night, calling for drink. Man has gone to ruin.

Jan 30th

Made port in Havana at last. Had run in with Union patrol who thought we were running for guns for the Confederates. Damnable war drags on in America. While we resupply, I am to visit my old friend Carlito. With luck he has interpreted the map. New engines are running well. Maybe's magic touch almost makes up for not having him here to run them. His loss is perhaps greater for the lack of his influence among the crew and with the likes of Gothe. Used even less coal than we imagined in the crossing, even with the delays, that I feel bodes well for the rest of the journey. I cannot hide my excitement. When we resume, we follow the route of the conquistadors. Oh, what grand adventurers we shall be.

Dearly, I would love to see Farnsworth's face when news of our success reaches London.

Feb 3rd

Gothe has made himself absent, most likely the man is drunk in one of Havana's dens of iniquity. Have lost patience with the man. To add to my woes, Carlito declined my invitation to accompany us. Declared it, 'A fool's errand', and I 'the fool'. Though he was jovial enough about it. My friend, I think, has gotten old and lost his taste for adventure. The easy life in Cuba has made him soft in his middling years. But he has confirmed the map is authentic in its antiquity, though whether it holds the truth or is some complex fiction he cannot say. Carlito has translated it in full, though the words are archaic in form and meter. The translation is beguiling in its vagueness, but between them and the map itself I believe the way may be found. Maybe's condensers will give us the advantage over the river. Maybe assured me that even the greenest sap wood would burn like coal. We set sail on the dawn tide, be there sign of Gothe or no. It pains me to see a man gone to such ruin, more so a friend and old companion. If he fails to appear, we shall leave him in Cuba. Perhaps in time he will find himself once more but I fear if the drink does not kill him, his temper in his cups will. Have written to Maybe on the subject, and expressed my regrets. After all, it was he entreated me to give Gothe this latest chance.

Feb 8th

Crossed the equator, with all the normal revelry. As it was, young Samson, the ship's lad's first crossing the men painted him blue, draped him in sail cloth and ropes, and declared him sea king for the day. But dark clouds spoiled the day and dark moods fill the night. Found Samson weeping in the galley gone midnight. Suspect the men may have taken things too far. Gave him a shilling and expressed my regrets.

Feb 12th

Saw two ravens on the port side funnel. What they are doing this far out at sea is any man's guess. Black tidings according to our Norwegian cook, birds of the battlefield sent for the dead. Have warned him against spreading such foolishness. Yet, I shall admit I felt a chill when those ravens watched me.

Feb 19th

The mouth of the Amazon lays before us. Wide and gaping like the jaws of some beast, ready to swallow up those who venture down its throat. The men saw an albatross flying south and took it as a good omen. Ever superstitious the sailor. I would mock them for it save I have felt a cloud over me since we left Havana. Carlito told me a Spanish proverb about the fountain.

'He who seeks the cure to lost youth, is sure to cease to age, for the dead grow no older.'

I laughed at this in Havana, it seemed a fine jest. Now I find myself dwelling on those words. Have busied Collain copying the map on the journey south. It is my intention to send it and this journal to Maybe, that he may keep it for my son Benjamin should I not return. Perhaps this dark mood will lift once we sail into the basin. The crew feels my discomfort. No Maybe, No Carlito, not even that drunkard Gothe. The crew feels alien to me, and I have grown to hate Collain, who complains daily. If it were not for my need of his cartography, I would put him ashore at the first town we dock. He is not a man made for adventure and makes me miss my old companions.

That proverb haunts me now, as I write this.

Feb 25th

We have made port at Porta Castile, from here on in our true journey begins. Resupplying goes well and we should be ready to leave port with the morning tide. Before then I shall visit the British Consulate in these parts, Charles Parker, a solid enough fellow, whom I know from our previous venture on the river. With him I shall leave packages to be sent back to England, into the keeping of Maybe, and letters for my solicitors, should we not return down river no later than one year hence. It is my hope of course that this package never be sent. Aside Collain's complaints, the crew are in good spirits as we prepare to brave the river. Helped, no doubt, with the prospect of an evening's liberty in the port. Though I have cautioned them against gambling and the dangers of whoring in a place such as this, I have little doubt some will return with no money, a dose of the pox or both. I will be glad if all of them return at all, Castile is akin to those new cities in the American west. A lawless place where a man's luck can turn on a card.

Tomorrow we sail for fame and fortune, or perhaps an ignominious fate. I wish as ever my Jane was with me, though what she would make of this venture I scare imagine. Am I a fool I wonder to seek the fountain? What hope does the secret of youth hold to the widower? Then again perhaps in seeking it, I shall instead find peace in finality and be reunited with my love in the hereafter. Perhaps that is the true adventure I seek.

"That's where the log entries end, save soundings, manifests and other such things," Benjamin told Eliza, having read them to her, though he skipped over the nautical lists of latitude and wind speeds and read only the extended notes for each day. Now he was finished, he looked up from the pages and saw her staring back at him. He was about to ask her what was wrong when she made her feelings abundantly clear.

"My father died for this… this… this nonsense?" she said to him, her voice full of exasperation. He could not blame her for that, it was, all somewhat ridiculous after all.

"I'm sad to say that seems to be the case."

"You're sad?"

"Yes, Miss Tu-Pa-Ka, I am sad and regret the death of your father. But…"

"But what Mr West? But what? Your father caused all this by sending those documents to mine in the first place.

Had he not done so my father would still be alive!" she snapped, though there was little bite to her words. He suspected she was not angry with him or even just raging in general, if anything she seemed instead to have gained some grim acceptance of events. Though if he had asked her, he suspected she would have told him differently. Perhaps she had become numb to it all. Rage can only burn so long before it leaves you hollow, he knew. Perhaps that is how she felt now, in the face of everything, he considered.

"I can only apologise for all of this," he told her.

"Oh, Mr West what use are your apologies? They won't bring my father back. Besides, what your father set in motion is… well, beside the point. He may have sent those documents to mine, but he had no hand in killing him. What I want to know is who did? Harrington wouldn't care a fig about something like this unless there was coin in it. Who was in the carriage, that's what I want to know? And how for that matter did they even know these documents existed?"

"Good questions all, ones I would dearly love to know the answer to," Benjamin admitted.

"How did you know my father had the documents in the first place?" Eliza asked after a moment's thought.

"I told you, I received a letter from the family solicitors, the one my father sent from Brazil."

"I see, and this letter was held by those solicitors for how long?"

"Fourteen years, I believe. It was kept until I reached my majority then given over to me."

"Fourteen years!" she said, sounding aghast.

"I know, but there were explicit instructions with it. It had to be withheld until my father was declared dead legally. Then there was some legal wrangling, assets held in a trust, legal statutes contested by investors, that kind of thing. It all got held up in the courts, an argument was made to declare all his assets forfeit to pay his debts," Benjamin explained.

"Why weren't they?" she asked.

"Because they weren't legally his as such. This house, all his investments and trust funds, they were all separate to his South American company. My grandfather saw to that, he is very protective of family money, that was the reason my father needed investors in the first place. Technically the only thing my father left me was the letter. His estate, this house, investments, everything I own. It all came to me via my grandfather, but that was contested anyway. Lawyers took their pound of flesh, it all was somewhat damaging to the family's reputation unfortunately."

"Oh, the troubles of the rich…" Eliza said, rolling her eyes a little.

Benjamin smiled painfully, her sarcasm hard to refute, but he found himself wondering if she knew the legal status of her own fathers' estate. There would be a will he suspected, Maybe Tu-Pa-Ka, from what little he had been able to gather, was not the kind of man to leave probate to chance. But a will meant dealing with solicitors, he did not envy her that. He had developed a healthy distaste for such men.

"Fourteen years," Eliza mused aloud, bringing him back to the matters at hand.

"What of it?" he asked, wondering why she brought that up of all things.

"Fourteen years… Don't you see…?" she retorted. But she clearly took the look on his face to mean he didn't and returned a look of frustration. "Have you always been this dim, Mr West?"

"I am afraid I don't follow you, Miss Tu-Pa-Ka," he replied curtly, causing her to sigh heavily, then explain as if she was speaking to a child.

"For fourteen years that letter was held your solicitor, and for the same fourteen years my father was holding the map and the logbook. Fourteen years and yet nothing happens. No one asks him about it, no one tries to obtain it from him, nothing, until you finally get the letter. Nothing at all. No one comes to my father trying to buy him off, no one comes threatening him either. Nothing happens at all, until you receive that letter."

"I'm still not sure what you're suggesting, Eliza," he said, and a smile crossed her lips, along with the slightest of laughs, she was clearly feeling pleased with herself. In return he felt something between annoyed and foolish that he could not grasp what she was getting at. He had never liked feeling a fool. If his face betrayed how he felt it only made her smile a little broader. She was enjoying his discomfort he was sure. He would have been more annoyed it wasn't for the way her eyes lit up a little when she smiled, he realised, and sighed heavily, returned a painful smile of his own.

"Someone else has read the letter, they must have done," she explained at last after making him wait something of an age.

"Impossible, it was sealed, and besides I have utter faith in my solicitors. They have been the family's firm for decades," he said, genuinely perturbed by the suggestion.

"Seals can be broken and then resealed," she said, making no effort to hide her tone.

"But still Hogarth, Hogg and Trench are entirely reliable, I assure you."

"Well, someone else read it, I'm sure. If not at the solicitors, then someone among your staff perhaps?" She let the suggestion hang between them, and then when he did not answer her eyes narrowed, "Have you always been such a lunkhead? Fourteen years pass, and nothing happens, then that letter is pulled out of a safe somewhere and lands on your desk. Then within a couple of weeks my father is dead. Fourteen years, Mr West…"

Benjamin realised she was probably right and found it shocking, which doubtless showed all over his face. It did not bear contemplating to him that either his staff or the family's firm would betray his confidence. But she was right, clearly right. He should have seen it himself. But it couldn't be the staff. There was only Mrs Bridge and her husband after all, and Alice and Sam were as good as family themselves. The only other member of staff was Gothe, and clearly the idea that he would have had a hand in this was patiently ridiculous. Which only left the firm…

"Perhaps you should read me the letter, Mr West." Eliza prompted.

"I'm not sure I…" he said, somewhat at a loss for words once more.

"Oh, for god's sake, read me the damn thing. I want to know what it says. Frankly, I feel I need to know what it says. It seems I'm the only one capable of rational detachment right now. So, read me it," she said with some of the tell-tale snappiness leaching back into her voice. The same take charge snap that she had shown back in the warehouse when removing the bullet from Gothe's back. Benjamin decided quickly it would be pointless to protest, besides which he felt a certain admiration for her when she spoke to him like that. So, despite his reticence, knowing as he did the contents of the letter and what it said about Miss Tu-Pa-Ka herself, he searched through his papers for the letter in question.

Then after a moment's pause to collect himself, he read it aloud to her.

To Benjamin Edward West

My son,

Should you be reading this, then I have not returned from this journey I am now undertaking. Porta Castile is the last fair port on the Amazon's tidal basin. From here on in we sail into the jungle and the wilds. The fountain, that which I seek, is no myth, I am sure of this. We found a map on a long dead conquistadores' corpse, on my last journey up this river. That map and my journal I have sent to my old friend Maybe, an engineer with his own works in Cheapside.

Maybe is a man I trust more than any other. He will be able to tell you more of all this when you are of age should you wish to know it. The last time we tried to do this journey our engines failed for want of good coal. This time Maybe's children will, I hope, take us further. Perhaps when I return, I shall be a young man once more, and have the means to a new fortune and the fame I have sought so long. Or else perhaps all this will be for nothing, but I have spent too many years pursuing this goal to balk at it now. I am committed to this undertaking, to this great adventure, but if you are reading this then perhaps it will have been my last.

My son, you were born too late. Both I and your mother were old to have children in the first instance but know that you were a child of love. The only love I have found in my long life. Yet fool I was, I was gone from one year to the next and did not see you grow into the man you may become. It was not your fault I chose this life. I found too painful were the memories of your mother's passing and your birth, and you always bring her to mind when I look upon you. Perhaps a younger me will be a better father to you, for I know I have been distant and aloof in more than merely the obvious ways. You deserved a better father, more than I deserved a son. But it is my hope you will perhaps forgive me my weaknesses. Know that I loved you, as I loved your mother and think not ill of me till you know great loss as I do.

Perhaps Maybe's Daughter will bring you here in my stead to seek my bones. For Maybe is sure of his daughter and perhaps it would have been wiser were I to have waited for her. I wish now I could see the wonder his daughter will doubtless be. If I have failed, I am sure with her you will succeed in my stead if you chose to do so. If not, I wish you well in whatever you make of your life.

Either way, the map and logbook Maybe holds will be yours now if I have not returned from this journey. Do with them what you will. I am sure you will be the finest of men. I commend you however to keep Maybe by your side, for I know no better man. Seek out his wisdom and aid. And, if he lets you, ride his daughter as I would have.

> *Your father,*
> *Edward Percival West*

Chapter Fourteen

The Visitation
of Sir Robert

Benjamin blushed when he read the last words out to Eliza. They were ridiculous after all. As ridiculous an instruction as any father could ever leave a son.

It was not, he admitted to himself, that he had any actual objection to the notation. Quite the opposite indeed, for all such thoughts lacked all sense of propriety. The encounter in his old bedroom earlier, which was of course an error on his part and indeed a terrible thing for which he was mightily ashamed and indeed sorry, had, it was hard to deny, left an impression upon him. She was a fine woman, both in strength of character and in terms of, well not to put too fine a point on it, she was more than merely comely. True, he found her company stressful, she had a way of switching between moods that made it difficult to know what to expect next from her. She also had none of the social graces he was used to when it came to conversing with women of his own class. Yet she exhibited none of the deference he had come to expect from the lower classes. He was not, he had admitted to himself, entirely sure what to make of her.

Also, when he had encountered her in the bedroom... Well, she had legs, quite remarkable legs... Legs he was finding it difficult to put out of his mind. They were quite distracting legs, and while he liked to present himself as a man of the world, his experience of the fairer sex was... Well, there had been that summer studying in Rome two years ago, but while he was not inexperienced, he was, though he was loath to admit it even to himself, not as worldly as he might be. He was unused to seeing a woman within his own house dressed only in a nightdress.

He had imposed on his housekeeper to lend Eliza a nightdress the night she had been brought to the house unconscious. But Alice Bridges was a little under five foot, while Eliza was closer to six. Consequently, the nightdress was a little short. So, as she had been leaning over the trunk when he walked in… Well, he really should have knocked first before entering, clearly. But well her legs, yes, he had noticed, she definitely had legs.

That is to say, he had always been aware she had legs. Clearly she had legs, and had always had legs, but well, the fact a woman definitely has legs beneath a dress that fell to her ankles, is not the same as a woman definitely having legs when a nightdress isn't even trying to cover her knees… He had been barely able to keep her legs off his mind for the last hour.

But still, he reminded himself, there was a difference between what went on in the privacy of a gentleman's own mind, and those last few words written in his father's letter. Words which were, well, positively indecent. He had only read them to her aloud out of completeness. Well, completeness may not be the right word. Again in honesty, to himself if no one else, he was perhaps hoping those words might, perhaps, spark a reaction of some kind from her. A reaction from which he could gauge, perhaps, what she herself may think of such an idea.

Well, a reaction was something he certainly received. Though not the reaction that a private part of his mind had secretly hoping for…

The reaction he received was laughter, long, hard, laughter.

Indeed, she was laughing so hard and loud, it was clear to him she found the whole idea as absurd as he, frankly, should. He did not take this as a good sign. Indeed, she seemed to find it so utterly laughable that in all honesty he felt slightly offended.

He grimaced, trying, and failing to hide his embarrassment. First, she laughs when he tells her the map showed the location of the fountain of youth. Now she laughs at his father's last words to him, even if those were admittedly a tad improper.

"Miss Tu-Pa-Ka, if you can contain your amusement," he said rather more sharply than he intended. But rather than recoil at his words she just laughed all the harder. He started to wonder if some form of delayed concussion was the cause. Some mild hysteria. He was aware the fairer sex were prone to such things, or so he had read in a recent scientific journal. She had taken quite a blow to the head, after all.

"Miss Maybe…" he said again, louder and trying to sound both firm and serious in equal measure, not realising as he did so he used her father's name. The name he had first known her by, and by which she had been commonly referred to back home in Cheapside.

Perhaps it was the use of that name which brought her up short, but Eliza forced herself to stop laughing, at least for a moment, and tried to collect herself. Then looking at West's puzzled expression, she could not help herself but burst back into a fit of laughter once more.

She was surprised at herself, but really it was too funny. What with everything that had happened in the last week, this was too funny by far. All the undealt with emotions she had piling up behind a dam of necessity burst due to his miscomprehension of his father's words. She needed to explain to him, she knew she did. But right at that moment the release of laughter was the medicine she really needed. No matter how uncomfortable it made Mr Benjamin West. Explanations, she decided, could wait.

"Miss May… Tu-Pa-Ka please…" West said again, and she looked away from him, forcing herself to cough to hide her amusement.

Right then she dared not look him in the eye. 'Ride Maybe's Daughter indeed…'

Before more could be said or she could get enough of a grip on herself to explain, there was a loud knocking at the door, which preceded it being opened and West's butler stepping in. At least Eliza assumed he was the butler, though he was not a man built for a butler's uniform. He looked more like a gardener forced into a suit when he would have rather been down among the rose beds. His hair was a mess of greying curls, and his face had the ruddy complexion of a man used to working outdoors.

The butler, who Eliza assumed rightly was Alice's Sam, cleared his throat diplomatically and Eliza covered her mouth to stifle further laughter. Coughing once more she forced herself to bring an end to her mirth.

"You have callers, Sir, Inspector Grace of Bow Street and a Sir Robert Peel. They request you attend them immediately. I have directed them to the front sitting room and Mrs Bridges is bringing them tea," Sam Bridges, butler cum odd job man said in a steady, if slightly disapproving, voice. He was not sure what the master and the young lady had been up to in the master's library, but he was sure that the amount of laughter he had heard at the door was something he, as butler, should disapprove of. He had waited a good minute for the laughter to cease, but as it seemed unlikely to end, he had made the uncomfortable decision to intercede. Sam was a man who liked a good laugh himself, but he felt that being disapproving was the thing for a butler to do.

In truth he had no idea if that was the case or not. He had not been butler for very long. Before the master took up residence at the town house, he and his wife had been employed as housekeeper and odd job man. Which for the previous five years had been a task not complicated by anyone being in residence. Indeed, he had had a side job down at the docks three days a week and took two more off entirely. The only actual resident other than themselves at the time had been Mister Gothe, who kept to himself in the cellar most days. As jobs went, it had been a good one, low paid admittedly, but it had included a couple of rooms in the attic for him and the wife to call their own.

He had been slightly put out, when Mister West had returned from his studies abroad to take up residence in the old family house. True, the young master had employed the two of them on superior wages as household staff. Jobs which had not proved to be overly arduous, as most of the rooms in the house remained mothballed. But Sam Bridges missed working on the docks, or more exactly, sloping off to the pub early and coming home to the missus late. He would admit, however, a butler's work was easier on the back than the dockside and it was nice warm inside work. He and the missus considered it a step up in the world. Particularly as one of his jobs as butler was to keep the liquor cabinet well stocked. Sam took good care of the liquor cabinet, and never let the risk be run that there would not be a good bottle of port or two in the house. Or that an open bottle would be allowed to spoil. However, for all his faults as a butler, Sam Bridges was a man who believed in doing a job properly. Hence, he had a mind to be disapproving when he thought that was what a butler should be.

He was also a mite flustered, he would happily admit, were he not doing his best butler impassive face. The last few days had been harder work than normal; he had barely had time to enjoy a bottle of port in the kitchen since the master returned from his latest venture with a mud-covered Mr Gothe in tow. Them and this odd slip of a girl who was definitely not a lady, no matter what his Alice called her.

He was all the more flustered right at that moment as he had had to deal with not only a police inspector for the second time in as many days, but a man he was almost sure was something important in the government. Though he was not entirely sure what 'The Home Secretary' actually did. He was certain it called for best china and tea to be presented with buttered scones, which had sent his wife into a bit of a tizzy.

Alice in a tizzy was a sight to behold in Sam's opinion. But a sight best beheld from the safety of the scullery, with a bottle in his hand, while employing a degree of selective deafness. Years of marriage had taught him that being seen to listen to his wife when she started talking was more important than actually listening to what she was saying. Alice Bridges did not talk to you, she talked at you, and when she was in a tizzy once she got a head of steam up, that talk could go on for hours.

"Sir Robert's here?" the master asked with a tone that suggested disbelief.

"Yes, Sir. Alice is waiting upon the gentlemen now," Sam replied, attempting to sound neutral on the matter, but it was hard to hide his chief concern, that being that his wife might forget herself and start talking at the gentlemen.

"I see. I shall be down forthwith," his master told him, with some alarm.

"Very good, Sir," Sam said and turned to leave.

"Robert Peel? Here. Why would the Home Secretary come here?" he heard the young lady asking as he left the room and found he was wondering the same thing himself.

The recent goings on worried Sam. Not least because he was getting used to a comfy life working for Mr West.

Sam Bridges smelt trouble looming and he did not much like the smell.

In, what he assumed was, the drawing room, Inspector Grace stood nervously holding a cup and saucer. He had been nervous all day, ever since his report on the incidents in Maybe's Manufactory and at Sheers Warf had despite all expectation, been read by people in authority. He had not expected the report to do much more than gather dust on the superintendent's desk after a brief once over by the old man. Instead he was summoned to the office by his superior and questioned repeatedly over one minor point in the report. Then a runner was sent to the Home Office. An hour later that runner had returned, noticeably out of breath, and Grace had been ordered to attend the Home Secretary at Westminster at 'his earliest convenience,' a polite phrase for immediately. Of course, on arriving at the Home Office he had spent three hours sitting in a side room waiting for Sir Robert to see him at Sir Robert's 'earliest convenience' which was defined differently.

Three hours sitting in a small room staring at the wall and no one offered him a cup of tea, let alone a bite to eat. It was frankly a disgrace.

Then he had been ushered into Sir Robert's office and asked exactly the same questions the superintendent had asked earlier that day. Questions about one name that appeared in his report that he had only included for completeness. Why that name had caused him to be dragged across town to wait on the Home Secretary's pleasure he had no idea. But it worried Grace, that was for sure. While it was true he had been hoping to be introduced to Sir Robert at some point, he had envisioned it would be for breaking a major case and being seen as a man to watch. Not because he put a name in a report that had been given to him by a witness who could not entirely be relied upon when it came to that name's veracity. A witness he had now accompanied Sir Robert Peel to call upon.

The ride to the West residence had been nerve-racking for Grace. He had sat silently trying to think of anything to say that would not mark him a fool. The Home Secretary had not helped by sitting in silence opposite him, reading Home Office papers from a dispatch box and tutting every few moments. Sir Robert seemed in a foul mood. Though Grace had no way to judge if it was a bad mood or just the manner of the man. Everyone knew Sir Robert had a temper and a reputation for being tempestuous at the dispatch box. He was, however, keenly aware that if this meeting went badly, he could find his career in tatters before the day was out.

So now as he stood holding his saucer and cup of slightly inferior tea in Mr West's drawing room, with an impatient Sir Robert Peel, he was dearly hoping that Mr West would be somewhat less laconic than he had been the last time they spoke. Indeed, he was starting to rue the day he had first been dragged into the whole mess down in Cheapside.

He was also rather worried about one thing both the superintendent and Sir Robert had insisted upon. That being that he had to apprehend the loathsome Harrington forthwith. Harrington who appeared to have disappeared without trace into Cheapside's slums after the gunfight at the wharf. It was, for some reason, a matter of national security. All very hush hush. So, it had to be handled with kid gloves, they had told him. How was he expected to do that? Finding Harrington would require kicking down doors in Cheapside and asking informants for information. How was he supposed to achieve that on the hush hush?

It really was all too much. It made him miss India and the damn mutiny.

"Sir Robert, Inspector, what brings you to my home at this hour?" Benjamin West said, entering the room with a look on his face that suggested he was not entirely comfortable with their appearance at his door.

Grace could not blame him for that.

He was followed in by his butler, who seemed entirely unsuited for the role, and by Miss Maybe, whose appearance was somewhat more surprising to Grace, though he was aware she was convalescing at the West residence. True, it was good to see she was not too worse for wear after the events at the wharf. Also, according to Perkins' rather confused reports, she had been instrumental in making sure both Mr West and the young copper had not ended up drowned in the Thames with their hands bound behind their backs. But what was West thinking bringing her with him to see the Home Secretary? Clearly, he did not grasp the gravity of the situation. She was, after all, a woman, and, well, not to put too fine a nib on it, a colonial. This did not bode well; it did not bode well at all.

"Mr West, a pleasure, Sir," Sir Robert stated, though his tone suggested this may not entirely be the case, but Grace was still unsure if this was just how the man was. "And you would be Miss Tu-Pa-Ka, I am given to assume," he added in slight soft tones, though Grace detected a hint of his own surprise in the Home Secretary's voice.

Miss Maybe looked somewhat taken aback by the use of her actual surname. As indeed was Grace, as that had not been in his report, though he had used her father's full name when noting the suspected link with his death. Sir Robert was clearly a good study.

"Sir Robert…" said the woman in question, though her tone suggested she was unsure of herself and what was expected from her as a greeting.

Grace felt for her. She was clearly a fish out of water in polite company, let alone that of a senior government minister. She managed a polite little dip that could be construed as a curtsy but hung back near the doorway. Grace suspected she did that so she could bolt if she felt the need. He envied her such an option.

"I must offer you my condolences and the condolences of Her Majesty's government on the loss of your father," Sir Robert said, with what sounded to Grace like genuine feeling. Not that he set much store by this. The man was a politician to the bones, he had to be to have risen so high in government circles. But he was sure Miss Maybe, at least, was fooled by this act of compassion.

"That is kind of you, Sir. His loss grieves me greatly," she replied politely.

"I'm sure. A terrible business, all of this, but the personal tragedy for yourself is greater still, I'm sure. If I or the Home Office can do anything for you, then please, just ask," Sir Robert said and Grace almost believed he was sincere.

"Arresting Harrington and sending him to dance the Tyburn jig would be acceptable," the woman replied earnestly, which caused Sir Robert to laugh. Actually laugh. He seemed genuinely charmed by the woman, much to the inspector's surprise.

"I assure you, we will endeavour to do just that, dear lady… Indeed, Inspector Grace here has been charged to do so," Sir Robert told her, much to the inspector's disgruntlement. He could have done without the reminder of the problems he was going to have with that dictate and the command that he should do so quietly. A caveat Sir Robert neglected to mention.

"Then I'm sure it is only a matter of time. I've every faith in the good inspector," she said, which was much to Grace's surprise, because she sounded quite genuine in her words. It was gratifying to be appreciated, so gratifying that it did not occur to him that she too might have some measure of a politician's guile about her.

"I shall do my best to apprehend the miscreant," Grace assured her, which received a nod of approval from Sir Robert, leaving Grace thinking that maybe this would all work out to the benefit of his career after all.

Then Sir Robert cleared his throat and became entirely serious once more. "But, now, dear lady, if you will forgive us, I must speak to Mr West here in private about matters surrounding the events of the last few days."

The merest flash of anger crossed the woman's features, and for a moment Grace thought she might argue. He would have understood if she had, she was after all tied up in the whole mess. He was glad, however, to see she thought better of berating the Home Secretary. Instead she gathered herself and curtsied once more to Sir Robert.

"Gentlemen, I shall leave you to your discussions," she said and departed, though the door had not quite swung shut behind her when Sir Robert mentioned the name that had brought him and the inspector to the West residence. The name that had made Grace's report such a hot potato and which had dragged politics into the whole affair.

"Now Mr West, tell me, what do you know about Michael Farnsworth?" the Home Secretary asked, with a grim overtone to his words.

Eliza was fuming. It was, frankly, ridiculous. She had as much right to be in that room as any of them. Whatever they had to say, it concerned her and what had happened to her father. She had a right to know. As for that name, Farnsworth... Who was Michael Farnsworth? What did he have to do with any of this?

She was half tempted to listen at the door, but the butler who was hanging about in the hallway in a most un-butler-like fashion would probably disapprove of her doing so.

The sooner she got back home to Cheapside the better. Then she could set about finding bloody Harrington and dealing with him before the police got in the way. Besides which, she would be doing them a favour. Inspector 'bloody' Grace would be lucky to find his backside with his elbow, let alone Harrington if he did not want to be found. West, damn him, was little better and would probably be less than useful in the long run. Oh, she was grateful to the man for getting her to a doctor and fixed up and all. But he was a rich twerp who would doubtless lose interest in her, and her troubles, soon enough now he had his blasted papers. If she did not leave, then before long she would be out on her ear, of that she was sure.

Out on her ear with a tattoo on her back that led to the fountain of bloody youth. That was a laugh, wasn't it? His nibs' mad old dad had run off to find a myth in the middle of the Amazon jungle, damn him as well. Dragging her father into his own madness by sending him a damn map to something that was impossible. And now, damn fool that she was, she had it freshly tattooed on her back. Whatever had possessed her to do that? Well, she blamed the grief. Everyone knows people do crazy things in grief, and clearly so had she.

To think I thought it might be a treasure map or something. Why else would people be after the damn thing if not for treasure. Not some mythical fountain of youth. Gods, men were stupid sometime... No, not sometimes... Men were always stupid, she thought, "Even you father..." she muttered to herself.

What the hell was he doing mixed up with a nutter like West's old man in the first place?

No, come to think of it, she knew exactly why he had involved himself in this madness. His damn daughter. It was his one weakness, she knew, his one passion. He would have done anything for his bloody daughter. No doubt he thought Mr West senior would invest money in her, and it looked like he wasn't wrong.

What was it Benjamin had read...? 'Ride Maybe's Daughter as I would have done...'

She had to stifle a laugh once more as she remembered the confused look on Benjamin's face, his clear misunderstanding. He had genuinely thought it was referring to her. She wondered what he would say when she explained what his father had actually meant.

She also found herself wondering if Benjamin had a head for heights.

Annoyed as she was by her treatment at the hands of the gentlemen, she still could not help but smile at that idea...

Then she saw Gothe standing in a doorway at the back of the staircase, waving her over. Oddly once he had caught her eye, he turned and without waiting to see if she followed him, he stepped back though the door, which she could only assume led down into the cellar.

Eliza watched him step down into the darkness of the stairway. She took a deep breath, still fuming at being sent from the room because she was a 'dizzy bloody woman'. Then shrugged to herself and followed Gothe down into the darkness...

"Michael Farnsworth, I was at Oxford with him. As far as I know he is at the Foreign Office now, I hadn't seen him for several years until three nights ago," Benjamin told Sir Robert as the door closed behind Eliza. He had a horrible sense she would make her feelings about being sent from the room known to him later, and that he would not enjoy her doing so.

"Did you know him well?" Sir Robert inquired.

"Sadly yes, I'd never call him a friend, but we did run with similar crowds at university though."

"And you are sure it was him?"

'Why, West, what an unwelcome surprise to find you here…'

Oh yes, he was sure. Despite all the other aches and pains from his adventures of the last few days, the kick in the ribs he had received from Michael Bloody Farnsworth still ached the most.

"Quite sure," he said coldly.

"I see… That's problematic, very problematic. Can I count upon your discretion, Mr West? There are things afoot that make these events you have found yourself involved in seem quite minor in comparison. Events that involve Mr Farnsworth."

"Really? Well, of course Her Majesty's government can rely upon me," Benjamin said with no reservation, if anything he was intrigued

"I'm not asking on behalf of the government, Mr West. But on behalf of the Home Office," Sir Robert explained.

"Are they not the same thing?"

"Usually, Mr West, usually. But not entirely in this case…" he was told, and the Home Secretary's eyes narrowed a little.

Benjamin thought on this, then a thought occurred to him and he risked half a smile. While he had little interest in such things, he was not entirely unaware of how politics worked.

"You think the Foreign Office is involved?" he asked. There was always friction between different branches of the government, but this sounded more than just civil servants jostling for position while their political masters played their games. If the Foreign Office was involved in the kidnapping and the attempt to drown him then he would make an exception to his normal lack of interest in affairs at Westminster.

"If only it were that simple, Mr West. Unfortunately, Mr Farnsworth is no longer with our 'friends' at the Foreign Office. Again I must ask you for your word that none of what I tell you will leave this room, yours and indeed your word as well, Inspector, or else I will have to remove you from the investigation, and I may have to have you transferred."

"You have my word, Sir Robert. The Home Office is of course the senior ministry, and whomever Farnsworth is involved with, well, events have set me against them, clearly," Benjamin reassured Sir Robert, then followed the minister's gaze as it fell on Inspector Grace.

"Transferred?" the inspector asked without meaning to phrase it as a question. Benjamin could tell the man was mildly horrified. Be it at the suggestion he would be anything less than loyal to The Home Office, or at the prospect that not being so would mean he might have to leave London, Benjamin could not tell.

"I am afraid so, Inspector. I can't have you stumbling further into this mess unawares, and I can't make you aware without your word," Sir Robert stated blandly, then added pleasantly enough, "I believe Lancaster is quite agreeable this time of year…"

"Lancaster…" said Grace, looking all the more horrified at the mere suggestion of being stationed in the north.

Sir Robert raised an eyebrow. The Home Secretary, famously, a Lancastrian by birth, clearly would not countenance bias against the county.

"A problem, Inspector?" he asked, and Benjamin detected just a hint of humour in the man's eyes.

Grace collected himself quickly and carefully phrased his response. "I will, of course, serve wherever the minister deems fit, but you can rest assured, Sir Robert, I'm your man in all things."

"Good, good. Well, gentlemen, as I say, none of this may leave this room. If word was to get out that there were rifts within the British government, I dare say our enemies would make haste to widen these rifts and set us against each other," Sir Robert explained.

"Ah yes, the colonial factions would be delighted, I'm sure." Grace put in.

"I was talking of the damn Liberals," Sir Robert snapped. "But yes, I suppose some dissatisfied colonials may seek advantage in any confusion, and the French no doubt…"

"Damn the French," Benjamin said with a smile. Such response was almost by rote even now fifty years since the last great battle of the Napoleonic wars.

"Quite…" Sir Robert agreed.

"So, if Farnsworth's not with the Foreign Office…?" Benjamin nudged.

"We believe he is working for The Ministry, Mr West."

"I thought you said he wasn't?"

"Wasn't what?"

"Working for the ministry, the Foreign Office…" Benjamin was now confused and feared he had missed something.

"I see. Perhaps I was unclear. He is no longer working for the Foreign Office, he is working for THE Ministry. The Temporal Histological and Esoteric Ministry. THE Ministry, you see…" Sir Robert explained.

Benjamin looked at Inspector Grace who shrugged his shoulders, then he looked back at Sir Robert Peel who appeared quite serious.

"Who in the blazes are they?" he asked.

The cellar was barely lit, and Eliza struggled to see beyond the steps in front of her. She was halfway down them when it struck her that following a walking dead man into a barely lit cellar was something that not many people would have considered wise.

If she was uncertain of Benjamin West, and she was, she was even more uncertain about Mr Gothe. Though she chided herself a little for that thought. Gothe had proved himself a loyal companion willing to risk life and limb... Well, limb at any rate... For West and indeed herself. He had stood alongside her on Sheers Wharf and she doubted she would have returned from the meeting with Harrington if he had not. Also, Gothe had saved her from shooting Harrington the first time, and much as she may claim she would have had no regrets about shooting the swine, doing so would have caused her more problems than enough, she was sure. It had been the strange not quite alive Mr Gothe who had stepped forward to defend her when the police came to visit as well. So, all considered if she was going to follow any walking dead man into a dark, slightly dank cellar, Gothe was the one she would choose to follow.

All the same, she could not shake the feeling she was making a mistake in doing so. For the hem of her dress if nothing else.

The lighting was no better once she got to the bottom of the steps, but she could see well enough to pick her way between stacks of boxes and travel trunks. She followed what could roughly be called a path through the layers of dust, until she got to a heavy wooden door reinforced with iron straps. It looked like a door designed to keep people out, or keep something in. Sturdy was the word that came to mind.

As she approached the door, it started to open, and despite knowing it was Gothe pushing the door from the other side, the atmosphere of the cellar made her nervous and a little jumpy. She found herself swallowing hard until the door was wide enough that she could see through it into a well-lit, remarkably cosy looking room beyond.

"Come through, Miss Eliza," Gothe said from beyond the door, and it wasn't until she passed through it that she realised he was standing at the far end by an empty fireplace. Nowhere near the door, which, after she passed beyond it, started to close behind her in a remarkably gentle fashion. It was all too creepy by far, so she made herself stop and look back at the doorway, half afraid she might find some other denizen of the cellar lurking in the shadows. Another living corpse perhaps, somewhat less appealing than Gothe…

"Ah, I see, pulleys," she said, looking at the mechanism above the doorway that was attached to a large crank wheel that drove a rod which pushed back and forth to open the door. No magic, no foul creature, just mechanics. She was at home with mechanics. Her eyes followed the drive belt, fascinated despite herself. It crossed the ceiling until it ended in a box next to a tall back armchair near where Gothe was standing, next to a pull cord, and she found herself wondering exactly how it was sprung to move so smoothly.

"Yes," Gothe replied with his usual stoic tones. "The rats drive them," he added.

She looked at him, half sure he was joking, though she could not remember him making any jokes previously, not as such. Then she let herself take in the room, which as cellars went was surprisingly well appointed. A large Persian rug lay before the empty fireplace, and the single high-backed chair rested beside a coffee table that looked like polished walnut. There was even a bookcase standing against one wall, though it was notable by its lack of books. But then Gothe did not strike her as much of a reader. Finally, pushed up against the facing wall was a large cot bed, with a locked seaman's trunk at its foot.

"You live here?" she asked and chose to ignore that she had just been invited into what was the bedroom by all appearances of a strange man, a very strange man in this case. Alive or dead, Gothe was definitely a man after all. Though thankfully she suspected whatever reason he had asked her to follow him it was nothing to do with any 'urges' he may have.

"Yes, Miss," Gothe replied and beckoned her towards him.

Her odd moment of apprehension on the stairs, and again at the door, had passed her now. She felt safe around Gothe. Besides he was as old as her father and had known him. So, she did as beckoned and walked over to him by the fireplace.

It was as she drew near his reason for bringing her down to the cellar became obvious. Faint though it was, the closer she came, the more obvious it became. She could hear voices. Voices that originated in the room above. The room with the fireplace that shared the same chimney stack as this one.

She nodded to Gothe, and smiled at him to show her appreciation, thinking to herself that this seemed about right. The men in the study were talking important business from which she was excluded due to her sex. While she was down in the cellar with a dead man, listening to every word they said, albeit those words a tad muffled. Yes, a woman was reduced to eavesdropping because men thought to exclude her. That was very much the way of the world she knew.

She heard Sir Robert Peel's voice say, "I see, perhaps I was unclear, he is not working for the Foreign Office, he is working for THE Ministry. The Temporal Histological and Esoteric Ministry. THE Ministry you see…"

"Who in the blazes are they?" West then asked.

Chapter Fifteen

The Machinations of Governance

"Two years ago, a man called Wells sought an audience with the Queen. Normally, of course, such audiences are restricted and carefully policed by the cabinet office. It wouldn't do to allow just anyone access to Her Royal Highness after all. Indeed, we're not entirely certain how he managed to get an invitation to a Royal Gala, or how he came to be seated so near the Queen herself. You see until two years ago, no one had even heard of this man, he appeared out of nowhere, in many respects a man without a past." Sir Robert explained.

"Perhaps an agent of a foreign power? A spy of some kind with a false identity?" Grace conjectured, his brow furrowed with concentration.

"Remarkably, Inspector, we members of Her Majesty's government are not entirely dim. We have considered such possibilities in some detail," Peel replied gruffly.

Benjamin had the good grace to cough to hide the inspector's embarrassment. Then he added some conjecture of his own, "I take it that no evidence could be found that that was indeed the case?"

"None whatsoever. He just appeared in London and purchased a house in Kensington, not far from here as it happens."

"He has money then? This neighbourhood is somewhat exclusive."

"Indeed, Mr West, though we have no idea where it comes from. He does not appear to bank with any reputable firm in the city."

"That is odd, but please go on. I'm sure his financial arrangements are the least of your concern."

"Indeed…" Sir Robert took a breath, considering his next words, as if he was weighing up just how much he should reveal. Then having reached a decision he ploughed on. "We, that is the Prime Minister and I, had put men to watching his house for several weeks after Wells first put an appearance in at the Palace. But it was when he somehow managed another invitation to the Palace a fortnight later, despite being put on a Home Office watch list, that we became truly concerned. The watch list should have prevented any repeat of the first instance. Yet somehow, he was on the guest list for an ambassadorial ball. And so, we took matters in hand and had men break into the house and search for any evidence he was working for the French, or the Russians, or the Americans for that matter."

"Hang on," the inspector interrupted, a shake in his voice, if not outright disbelief. "Are you saying that the government burgled a private citizen's residence? I mean, watching the man's house is one thing, but actually trespassing on his property?"

Benjamin raised an eyebrow at this odd bit of naivety in a copper. He himself had no illusions as to what the Home Office may or may not get up to in such circumstances.

"National security, Inspector! It was a matter of national security. This man had gained unfettered access to the Queen herself. We had every reason to believe he was a danger to the crown and the nation itself. Frankly it was the least we would do," Peel insisted.

Grace coughed himself this time, it was clear to Benjamin that the inspector was all too aware he was making a bit of a fool of himself. "Forgive me, Sir Robert. You are, of course, correct; the Queen and the nation must come first. I was merely surprised, that was all. Forgive me," he said quickly, and Sir Robert nodded to him with a modicum of respect.

"Indeed. Unfortunately, however, the men we had set to the task found nothing incriminating."

"Not even the items you'd had placed there the night before by the first burglar to give you cause to bring the man in for questioning?" Benjamin asked, with a slight laugh to his voice.

"Mr West, I hardly think Her Majesty's government would…" Grace started to say, and it was Sir Robert's turn to cough loudly.

"As you say, Mr West, not even those items we placed there ourselves. Indeed, our men found remarkably little. The papers we had arranged to be found were absent from the drawing room. And further investigation led our men to believe that this Wells wasn't even living in the building. The beds had never been slept in as far as they could determine. The kitchen was bare of actual food. No clothes graced any of the wardrobes. There were no servants either, which was one of the first things our men watching the residence had discovered. Wells was often seen coming and going, but only when he wished to be seen. We were quite certain the house was as much a front as the identity of Wells himself."

"Surly you could pick him up at any time?" Benjamin asked.

"Just pull a man off the street without good reason? This is hardly the colonies…" Grace said, but what should have been a righteous fury was more of a righteous whimper. Benjamin suspected the inspector had had more than one felon picked up by his officers on scant evidence. But East End louts were one thing, if this Wells was a gentleman of some kind, even a spy, a different set of rules would doubtless apply.

"Inspector Grace, this will go much simpler if you accept that Her Majesty's government at times engages in exercises that are less than palatable to a civilised man, in order to maintain the very civilisation in which he flourishes. Particularly in the case of agents of foreign powers seen as a threat to Queen and country…" Sir Robert said, with a withering tone.

Grace swallowing hard but he nodded his assent rather than further his interruptions. Benjamin suspected this was for no other reason than that Sir Robert was his boss at the end of the day.

"In any event, Mr Wells proved to be singularly elusive. To the extent that he seemed to know where and when we planned to scoop him up and manage to absent himself each time. It was, I will willingly admit, quite vexing."

"I'm sure, Sir Robert. But if I may, what has this odd character to do with The Temporary History and Egotistic, or whatever, Ministry? And Farnsworth for that matter?" Benjamin asked. Interesting though he was finding the discussion, he was eager to find out where it all fit in to recent events.

"The Temporal Histological and Esoteric Ministry, Mr West, and quite simply Wells founded it," Sir Robert explained.

"How is that possible? If he is as you suspect a foreign agent? How does a foreign agent found a government ministry?" Benjamin asked.

"How indeed…? That is frankly not entirely clear. That he had managed to gain the ear of the Queen after several appearances at the Palace was obvious to us, but to what end we knew not. Then when the Prime Minister visited the Queen a few months later for his weekly audience, he received instructions that a royal charter had been signed for the formation of THE Ministry and Mr Wells had been appointed as the minister of the crown with direct control of this new body," Peel explained, much to the surprise of his audience.

"I'm no expert," Benjamin said, while trying to get his head around this intelligence, "but can the Queen actually do that? I laboured under the understanding that all government ministers were appointed by the PM. The Queen can't actually appoint anyone as such. She charges the leader of whichever party is in power to form a government and that's about it, isn't it?"

"Yes, and no. Technically all ministers are appointed by the crown, and all ministries hold a royal charter. The crown is the seat from which all power flows, you see. It's true in normal circumstances the Queen appoints the Prime Minister and he appoints the rest. But constitutionally she does have the power to appoint her own. She merely never exercises that power... Or never had previously. Believe me my friend, the Prime Minister was quite put out when this occurred, but technically as he and indeed we all, serve at her pleasure, frankly, it was difficult to say no to the woman. I believe they had quite a heated debate on the subject..."

"I bet they did," Grace muttered, looking decidedly aghast.

"Indeed, but as she threatened to dissolve parliament and force a general election if he didn't agree to her request, in the end he had little choice but to do so. Numbers in the commons are remarkably even and frankly we've no idea who would win an election if one was called."

"So, this Wells is now a minister with his own ministry? But surely that means he now reports to the PM?" Benjamin asked.

"You would think so, would you not, but no THE Ministry operates entirely autonomously. Outside the control of the cabinet office and frankly we have no idea what they are up to. And believe me we've tried to find out.

But every spy we've tried to place in their offices at Mornington Crescent has been discovered in a matter of hours. They recruit quite independently of the normal channels, and Wells has been systematically undermining the government ever since. The Foreign Secretary for one now receives most of his instructions from the Crescent."

"How does that happen? Surely the PM can just sack the minister?" Grace inquired.

"You're not in politics, are you, Inspector? The Foreign Secretary is more popular with the party right now than the PM. He can't sack him, and he refuses to step down or be moved to another post. No, this Wells chose his patsy well and as I say, we've no idea what his end game is. Though some of the foreign policy decisions he has influenced have been remarkable."

"Remarkable how?" Benjamin asked, finding it all far more fascinating than he would have credited, he had never cared a great deal about politics in the past.

"Frankly, that's the rub. Everything the Foreign Office has done in the last several months has been a success, they have manipulated events abroad to the nation's advantage, quite remarkably in fact." Sir Robert told them.

Benjamin smiled slyly, feeling he had grasped at an important aspect of all that was been explained. "I see, and that has made the Foreign Secretary…"

"More popular with the party than ever, yes… Frankly we expect him to make a bid for the leadership in the next few months and in all likelihood he'll succeed." Sir Robert said with a grim tone.

"Surely not. The PM is well liked," Grace injected.

"By the voters perhaps, but within the party not so much. No Prime Minister ever is. There are always those who become disaffected. Men who feel that a new leader will give them the chance to rise that has been withheld from them by the current incumbent. You cannot run a party, let alone a government without making enemies. The PM's grasp on power is more tentative than it would appear," Sir Robert told them, and everything fell into place for Benjamin. Sir Robert's own political fortunes were clearly tied to the Prime Minister's. Probably more so than any of his fellows. He was seen by many as the heir apparent or had been certainly. A shift in power towards the Foreign Secretary did Sir Robert's career prospects no favours.

"I see, so Farnsworth was with the Foreign Office but is now working for this new Ministry, I take it?" Benjamin inquired. It was the obvious conclusion at that point. He had a fair idea why criminals and skulduggery were involved as well. Sir Robert held the keys to the kingdom in some respects, the police and the courts were under his mandate. This Wells character could not act directly within the country itself without Peel on side. Not legally at any rate. But he could act surreptitiously through well-placed bribes and by using underworld figures like Harrington. Manipulating things beneath the gaze of the Home Office.

"Yes, Mr West, so we believe, though until he showed up involved in the events in Cheapside we had no idea what he, or they were doing. It's a stroke of luck you recognised him, now we know they are up to something beyond meddling in foreign affairs. It does of course rather beg the question, what was it they wanted from you and Miss Tu-Pa-Ka?" Sir Robert asked, making his interest clear at last.

"I see, well ultimately what they were after was a map."

"A map? A map to what, Mr West?" the Home Secretary asked, bristling somewhat.

"Frankly Sir Robert, I suspect you're really not going to believe me when I tell you…" Benjamin told him, not least because he still was not entirely sure he believed it himself…

To Benjamin's surprise, Sir Robert's reaction to the news that a rogue section of the British Government had been attempting to secure a map to the fountain of youth was not utterly dismissive, incredulous, or even mildly disbelieving.

Instead the Home Secretary simply said, "I see…"

A reaction which sparked a degree of incredulity in Mr West.

"You see?"

Inspector Grace, whose reaction, to judge from the look on his face was incredulous on both counts, said nothing.

"Yes, Mr West, I see. We at the Home Office are privy to a great many things. We know, for instance, that fifteen years ago your father and grandfather had a disagreement over your father's plans for his latest, and what was to be his final expedition. Your grandfather refused him the use of family money, as I'm sure you are aware. This forced your father to seek alternative funding for his venture. As such, he created a private share scheme and approached several wealthy and, it should be noted, elderly individuals, offering exclusive access to what he hoped to discover in South America. His entire South American Company was financed on the promise of this 'fountain'. He was, I am given to understand, quite oversubscribed when he set off on his venture…"

Benjamin remembered only snippets of his father, and those through the lens of childhood, but nothing he knew about his father suggested he was a great salesman. "Surely no one truly believed he could find such a thing?" he said, incredulous.

"How old are you, Mr West?" Sir Robert asked him.

"I was twenty-five this April."

"I see, then perhaps that is why you don't understand how he managed to raise the funds he needed. Never underestimate the promise of renewed youth, Mr West… A great many rich men would've paid far more than they did for such a promise. Indeed, we are far from sure just how oversubscribed your father's venture was. When he disappeared on the Amazon more than one of those investors believed he'd done a runner with the money. They wrote letters to The Times and to my predecessors at the Home Office, demanding something was done. And of course, everything that could be done was done. It just so happened everything that could be done amounted to nothing. The Foreign Office has had a standard bulletin in every consulate and embassy they run stating that should your father show up he is to be detained and sent back to England. Some very important people invested in his venture, some of whom are still alive. I'm surprised you were unaware…"

"Well, I was aware my father's reputation was… colourful. But that was all."

"Yes… well your uncles and grandfather have done much to keep the scandal from breaking. Several leading investors received some small percentage of their investment back in return for their silence, or so I believe. Others were advised just how much the West family had invested in various companies, and how they may feel obliged to withdraw their interests if silences were not kept. Your family really is quite wealthy, after all. Such wealth buys a lot of silence, one way or another," Sir Robert explained, which made Benjamin slightly uncomfortable. Discussions of his family's money always did.

"But it did not buy enough silence, I'd venture," Inspector Grace put in, voicing a suspicion that had just started to cross Benjamin's mind, and he realised the earlier suspicions voiced by Eliza about the West family solicitors seemed all the more insightful, as Grace continued, "You say there was a map and some other papers of your father's. Items that were left in the keeping of Miss Tupar… Miss Tu-Parka… Miss Maybe's father. Well, clearly this Wells character knew of your father's expedition and had knowledge of the map's existence. Why else go to such elaborate lengths to secure it. For him to know of it someone else must have known and been more than willing to talk. Someone who invested in the original venture, I would posit, a someone as lured by the prospect of youth as they were fifteen years ago. This Wells learns of this and discovers the whereabouts of a map. Everything else follows on from there. Only thing to figure out is his own motive in wanting it."

"Why, Inspector Grace, I do believe you have put your finger on the pulse of the matter," Sir Robert said, sounding mildly surprised at the inspector's insight. "The why in this case is obvious however, Wells seeks leverage with the Queen. If, unlikely as it may be, there is any truth to this 'fountain of youth' then in obtaining it he would gain all the leverage he could ever need. The man who could hand youth to Her Royal Highness… Such a man would control the crown. Control the crown and you control the empire. Besides this does tie in with some of the rumours we have managed to piece together in regards to how Wells managed to worm his way into her Highness's good graces…"

'I see," said Grace.

"Be all this as it may, the question we have to ask ourselves, gentlemen, is what we do about it. How do we set about derailing this Wells character?" Benjamin asked.

"That is a matter for the government, Mr West, not private individuals like yourself," Sir Robert said primly.

"Damnation to that, Sir Robert. Before all this happened, all I was seeking was a way to find out what really happened to my father. This Wells character has stolen my property, caused a friend of my father's to be murdered, threatened his daughter and even tried to have me killed. I shall not be standing idle…"

"I see. Well, I can only caution you against further involvement. Sadly, there seems little to be done. We have no proof of this skulduggery, and now Wells has the map we have no idea what he will do with it, or indeed where it leads beyond somewhere in South America. The arm of the Home Office is, I assure you, long, but it isn't quite that long."

Benjamin must have been pacing the room above. His footfalls had an ominous quality to them, he was angry, she could tell. Her father used to stomp around in much the same way when vexed. Having listened to all that had been said, all be the words muffled slightly, Eliza was angry herself. She had determined that she wanted to see this H G Wells strung up for her father's death, even if she had to tie the noose herself.

She was also angry with Benjamin, though that was a more abstract anger. She knew he could not be held responsible for all that had happened, but at the same time had it not been for him and his father none of the misfortune of recent days would have befallen her.

And all for a dream, a myth, a bloody silly story only believed by bloody silly men. *Fountain of youth my arse*, she thought bitterly. And all for power, wasn't it always about power when it came down to it. British power at that, which meant British upper-class power. Politics, a festering wound in the side of society and who was to pay for all this politicking? Men like her father, honest hard-working men. Not that working men were much damn better…

A minute or two passed of Benjamin's pacing about, she wasn't sure how she knew it was him doing the pacing, but she was sure it was. Then abruptly he stopped as if the pacing man had reached a decision of some kind, he stopped and started talking once more.

"The thing is, Sir Robert, they don't have the map, not the whole map…" he said, and Eliza felt a bubble of anxiety in her chest. *Why would he tell the Home Sectary that of all things*, she thought, angrily.

"They don't?" Sir Robert asked, clearly surprised by this revelation.

"No, they do not." Benjamin said, and she could almost hear the smile on his face. Hear the smile and feel the knot in her stomach, knowing what he was going to say next and fearing it. "Thanks to our good friend Miss Tu-Pa-Ka they don't, she doctored the map before she handed it over to them,"

"Did she now?" Sir Robert asked, a note of slyness in his voice. "Clever girl… Clever, clever girl…" there was the sound of a begrudging laugh before he asked the question Eliza feared most. "I suppose it would be too much to ask for that she took a copy at all?" *Don't say it, don't say it*, thought Eliza, feeling flustered, but not so flustered that her anger was not further fuelled by the Home Secretary's 'clever girl' comment.

"As a matter of fact," she heard West say… And felt an overwhelming urge to slap the man, "she tells me she did just that," and the smugness with which he said it just twisted the knife in her guts.

"Clever girl indeed!" she heard Sir Robert exclaim, and it was the condescending nature of the surprise in his voice which pushed her over the edge.

She looked over at Gothe; big, strong and as passive as a tree trunk, and noted while his expression remained as bland as ever, even he was rolling his eyes. Flustered to the point of exhaustion with the stupidity of men she leant into the fireplace and yelled up it, doubtless to the surprise of the men above…

"It's woman, Sir Robert. Clever WOMAN!!!"

Chapter Sixteen

Whitehall Revelations

Three days later Benjamin was sat with Eliza, feeling less than entirely comfortable in her company, on a not entirely comfortable chair, in a small waiting room on the third floor of the Home Office buildings at King Charles Street in Whitehall. He suspected she was not feeling any more comfortable in his company than he was in hers. Though the chairs were certainly not helping matters.

They had conversed little over the previous three days, though Eliza had remained at the West's London residence by mutual agreement while she further recovered from her wounds. She had grudgingly conceded to his insistence that the machine shop in Cheapside was far from the safest location right at that moment, what with conspiracies within the government, Harrington still in the wind and several other matters up in the air, but she had made it plain she was far from happy with the situation.

Neither was he.

Eliza, he suspected, was unhappy because she felt she was under some form of house arrest. The Home Secretary had, it was true, only hinted that he would prefer 'that she remained with Mr West for the time being'. And as Benjamin mistakenly pointed out there were worse places to be confined to than a Kensington town house. He had added that his home afforded soft beds, an abundance of good food, and fireplaces that remained lit day and night. Though this, he would concede, had much to do with the diligence of Sam Bridges who might know little about being a butler but knew all there was to know about keeping the home fires burning. Confinement was, however, confinement at the end of the day and it was clear to him that Eliza was swiftly going a little stir crazy. She had told him, in no uncertain terms, she was a woman used to being busy, ill-suited to idleness.

Benjamin on the other hand was mostly unhappy with the arrangement because Eliza was so forthright in making her own unhappiness known. As a bachelor, he was unused to dealing with a woman about the place. Other than Alice Bridges, but the help didn't count, mostly because he hardly noticed them. Eliza, however, had a way of not speaking to him that was extremely noisy. Doors had a habit of being slammed. Cutlery clattered down on plates. And it astounded him how often she was wherever he wanted to be, only to dramatically leave the room upon his arrival. For a woman doing her best to avoid him, she seemed to always be right there.

Finally, it was a relief of both of them, he suspected, when the long-awaited summons to Whitehall had arrived. Though he also suspected that Eliza, who was fidgeting on the chair beside him, was quite as nervous about the meeting as he was. Possibly more so. She had after all quite vehemently admonished the Home Secretary in the West's drawing room. Insisting she would not reveal the location of her copy of the map to him or Benjamin for that matter until she had certain assurances. When they had asked what these assurances were, she had demurred somewhat and told Sir Robert he would have to wait for those as well. Sir Robert had left shortly afterwards with the inspector in tow. His final words to Benjamin had been quite abrupt, along the lines of, "Get that woman in line…"

This had frankly not helped anyone as he said them with Eliza in spitting distance.

After that Eliza had then informed Benjamin she was going to rest as she was feeling, 'all faint with all the excitement, I do declare,' which given the tone she used, an accent so posh it didn't so much cut glass as dare it not to part of its own accord, he suspected was not entirely honest of her.

The next three days a dark mood had come over the West household as he and Eliza had become embroiled in a battle of wills that involved not speaking to each other except in terms of the utmost politeness. She, he determined, was not about to forgive him for telling Sir Robert about her copy of the map. A subject she had, while patiently not talking to him, 'talked' to him about at length.

He had taken to spending time with Gothe down in the cellar, which he despised as it always felt damp even though it was not, and his former manservant never lit the fire because 'The dead don't feel the cold' as Gothe had told him once. He was somewhat suspicious of this pronouncement as Gothe always wore his heaviest coat even in the middle of summer... But such was his desperation to avoid the clearly angry woman who had become a permanent house guest. At least until the whole mess with Harrington was sorted out.

Yet despite his misgivings about Eliza's extended presence in his home Benjamin had also found himself seeking her out to check on her wellbeing whenever possible. He had told himself this was just because it was required of him to be a good host. Though he was not quite fool enough to believe that himself and neither, he suspected, was she.

The whole situation had not lent itself to much discussion on their situation, the contents of Benjamin's father's log, or the strange conspiracy they had both been dragged into. A lack of discussion which had persisted as they sat at opposite sides of the carriage as Gothe drove the carriage it across town to Whitehall, and which remained absent as they sat next to each other waiting on the Sir Robert's pleasure.

After half an hour of sitting there carefully saying nothing to each other, Benjamin was starting to feel the strain. He was about to resort to mentioning how unseasonably pleasant the weather was being. A sure sign of desperation on his part. Eliza, it seemed to him, was just as uncomfortable, but for her part seemed stubbornly determined to be utterly polite, which just made everything worse somehow.

Eventually when a clerk appeared, informed them the Home Secretary was ready to see them Benjamin's relief was palpable. Not that he was looking forward to the meeting but it did mean he would be in a room with someone else Eliza was mad at.

Sir Robert welcomed them in and sent the clerk off in search of the tea woman with instruction to secure a pot of Earl Grey and three cups. The clerk seemed unperturbed by being given a seemingly demeaning task, so Benjamin assumed this was a code to signify the Home Secretary wanted to have a private discussion.

"Sir Robert, a pleasure to see you again," Eliza said as they entered with consummate manners, which only worried Benjamin more.

"As it is for me to see you, my dear Miss Tu-Pa-Ka," the minister replied.

"Sir Robert," Benjamin said, offering his hand, and shaking, before taking to his seat as the Home Secretary took his. They had both been sitting a good few moments when Benjamin realised their error, He locked eyes with Sir Robert who had gone slightly pale, suggesting he had come to the same conclusion. They had committed a cardinal faux pas. Eliza remained standing by the chair beside her.

Benjamin saw that Sir Robert was as aghast as he was at their collective lack of manners. It was all the worse because while as host Sir Robert felt he should have pulled out the chair for his visitor, while Benjamin as the one accompanying Eliza arguably should have been the one doing the honours. Furthermore, as Home Secretary, Sir Robert could hardly be expected to come around to the other side of his desk to pull out a chair for a visitor, but as a gentleman he had no option but to do so for a lady. Whether Miss Tu-Pa-Ka counted as a lady when it came to societal manners was of course also a matter open to debate. She was not technically a lady of society after all. Frankly the whole thing was a minefield of social etiquette. Something of which, Benjamin was uncomfortably aware, Eliza knew perfectly well.

She was in short, Benjamin realised, playing them both like a fiddle.

Both men stood, rather too rapidly. Sir Robert started to round the table, but Benjamin raised a hand to dissuade him and stepped across to pull the chair out for Eliza. She was doing her best to appear bored and uninterested in the whole affair, which Benjamin knew was an act, he was sure she was secretly laughing at both of them.

In spite of himself Benjamin was impressed; he had met finishing school debutants who could not have pulled off that expression of bored disinterest quite so well.

Eventually, when they were all seated, the actual meeting could start at last. But he, and he suspected the Home Secretary were firmly of the opinion that they had just been put in their place by the 'slip of a girl' before them. Then he found himself reassessing that opinion and replacing the words 'slip of a girl' with 'woman' rather swiftly, feeling slightly uncomfortable about the whole affair.

He caught sight of the whisper of a smile cross Eliza's lips and suspected she had not enjoyed herself so much in days.

"So, Sir Robert, what's new in regard to Farnsworth, and the rest?" Eliza asked. Which dispelled any doubt in Benjamin's mind as to just how much of the conversation between gentlemen she had being privy to three days earlier.

"Ahem!" Sir Robert stage coughed, giving her a hard stare. "These are matters of state, Miss Tu-Pa-Ka, I am afraid I cannot make you privy to such intelligence as we have…"

"Oh, balderdash, Sir Robert, we already know the pertinent facts. A power struggle is underway, and you fear you may be on the losing side, beyond information I…" She paused and looked sideways at Benjamin for a moment then corrected herself, "That is we… hold, you've very little idea what the other side is up to. Luckily for you that other side had a hand in the death of my father and sought property bequeathed to Mr West by his. In short, while you may dance around a little and withhold what you can, you will tell us what we wish to know, because that is the only way you will get the information from us that you need. Is that not the size of it?"

Benjamin was shocked by the brazenness of his companion. He knew she was right. One look at Sir Robert's face, which was one part angry and two parts aghast, told him that. It was exactly the look a schoolboy might have had when he was caught red-handed in a lie. He reminded himself that Eliza was not a society lady, but a woman who had grown up in a Cheapside engineering shop. Doubtless she was used to dealing with stubborn men in a rather direct fashion. Sir Robert, if he had any doubt, was clearly discovering much the same. And judging by the way the Home Secretary's moustache was bristling, he was not entirely comfortable with being spoken to in such a direct manner by a woman, if indeed by anyone.

"Ahem," he coughed again, then his eyes, while not quite disguising his anger, softened a tad. "Quite, madam, quite. I shall be direct then. We, that is the Home Office, require the map you profess to have in your possession. We will pay you for it of course, if you would be so kind as to name a sum."

"It is most certainly not for sale, Sir Robert," Eliza replied stiffly.

"And if I insist?"

"I'm afraid you can't, Sir Robert…" she said, and for a second it looked like he was about to protest. But she raised her hand slightly to indicate she had not finished speaking, then continued. "However, I may be amenable to a bargain of sorts, indeed one that will be to our mutual benefit, I'm sure."

"And how would that be, Miss Tu-Pa-Ka?" he asked, clearly interested in what she may have in mind. Too interested, in Benjamin's opinion. The Home Secretary had been wholly too quick to grasp the olive branch, either he was playing with Eliza, or he was just a little desperate. He could not tell which.

"I wish to know exactly where our mutual enemies are and what they are up to. Oh, don't look so shocked that a woman would talk this way. We know more about having enemies than any man ever will. The whole of society is set against members of my gender from birth. This is a man's world, Sir Robert, as it always has been, because men made it that way. I'm an unmarried woman whose father is dead. I'm as good as a target for any man. I may well have inherited my father's goods and holdings but fat lot of good it will do me." she told them earnestly. Then after taking a moment to gather her thoughts she continued.

"No bank will deal with me. No tradesman who values his reputation will deal with me either. Within a few months I'll have to sell off everything just to pay the bills, and I've no doubt, for all the love in which my father was held, back in Cheapside, the wolves are already gathering around the corpse of his business, slathering to cheat me out of everything they can. If I stay unmarried, that is exactly what will happen. Within a month my few remaining friends will be telling me to find a husband. Oh, and I will have no shortage of offers, because everything I own would go to them in the marriage, because it's a man's world, Sir Robert. While the longer I wait, the less will remain with which to tempt some fat idiot of a man, a man not fit to lace my father's boots, let alone work his shop, to take me for a wife so he can get his hands on it all. Wait too long and I will be destitute, without protection and thrown to the wolves in the damn workhouse. A poor man in this country has it hard, Sir Robert, but the poor women of this nation have it worse than any men by tenfold… and I'll not find myself in that damn place. I've nothing but enemies, Sir Robert, every damn man in the world is my enemy right now. Even you, even Mr West here. Because it's a man's damn world. But, I tell you this, chief among all those enemies are the bastards whose scheming led me to this when they raised their hand against my father. So, I will do all I can to bring about their downfall. Is that clear? Now, I wish you to tell me what you know of them, and then who knows, if they are entirely lucky, you might get to them before I do…"

Benjamin was somewhat aghast, and from the look on Sir Roberts face he was not alone in feeling so, neither had dared interrupt her diatribe, nor did he feel he could contradict her words. Benjamin felt somewhat ashamed into the bargain, for he had never considered what Eliza's position would be now her father was dead. He doubted the Home Secretary had either. Indeed, while Benjamin had always considered himself to be a progressive, he had never really considered the lot of women as laid bare by Eliza just then.

"I've no wish to be your enemy, Miss Tu-Pa-Ka," Sir Robert said, after a moment's consideration, and somewhat softly it seemed to Benjamin. "Indeed, I dare say I pity those who are," he added with a grim smile.

"Then be my ally and let me be yours, but to do that you will have to take me into your confidence and do so without all this foolishness about things you can and cannot say in front of a woman."

Benjamin smiled to himself, as Sir Robert seemed to squirm slightly. He had a suspicion the Home Secretary had just been out manoeuvred quite deliberately by Eliza. He was certain that Sir Robert had been talking about both of them when he claimed there were things he could not tell them. But by making it all about her as a woman, she had steered the man into a position where he almost had to oblige her curiosity or end the meeting, and as he clearly needed the map that Eliza had squirreled away somewhere, the latter was not an option.

"Very well, but I must once more demand the word of both of you that what I tell you is treated with the utmost confidence," Sir Robert said after a moment of deliberation.

"Of course, you have it," Eliza stated briskly.

"And mine, Sir Robert," Benjamin added.

"Very well, we believe we may already be too late. We have been aware for a while that the Foreign Office, as a proxy for THE Ministry, chartered a vessel two months ago, which has been sitting at Southampton dock since then, being outfitted for an expedition. Until three days ago we had no idea what that expedition might be. Now I suspect it is to follow in the footsteps of your father, Mr West."

"That makes a dreadful kind of sense," Benjamin said.

"How so?" Sir Robert asked, though Benjamin suspected he knew the answer to that quandary and was just testing their powers of deduction.

"They've been after the map and my father's documents for weeks. They tried to buy them first, then tried to leverage them with threats, then finally they resorted to more direct methods, as we know. They had to have been preparing for this a while. Eventually they made an open move. To wit; a murder and then kidnapping. They wouldn't have done so unless they had all their ducks in a row. Otherwise once they showed their hand, you would be in a position to move against them."

"Indeed, that was our thinking, which was why we dispatched men to take custody of the ship yesterday. Unfortunately, that was a day too late. It sailed on the dawn tide, before my men even entered Southampton. Farnsworth, Wells and several others we've had under watch have all vanished in the last two days. All aboard that ship, I don't doubt. We have in effect missed the boat. Whatever they are afoot, and I think it is safe to assume it involves your father's map, they are now about it. Which leaves us few options. One of which involves your map, Miss Tu-Pa-Ka, and the hopes a fast frigate might intercept them. But even that is doubtful as frankly we have no idea which captains we can trust."

"Surely the navy is loyal to the government?" Eliza said, her surprise evident in her voice.

"Of course they are, but you forget, our foes are as much a part of the government as the Home Office, and short of the Prime Minister, the Foreign Office and through them THE Ministry have as much influence over the War Office as we at the Home Office do. More in actuality, we deal with matters at home after all, and the military primarily operate abroad."

"But the Prime Minister…"

"Is at heart a politician, who knows which way the wind is blowing. While he is still in our camp, he may well baulk at us openly using the military. Certainly, he will not wish to be publicly seen to take sides against the Queen's new minister of state, this Wells chap. Not while Wells enjoys the Queen's favour. While we could move against them surreptitiously here, overt moves against them will not be allowed. Frankly I want to see the map now only to see what we might do to prevent them reaching their goal, if it is this damn fountain, which frankly I doubt. More likely it is some map to lost Spanish treasure left over from the conquistadors or some such thing. I always believed the whole fountain of youth thing to be just a smoke screen for something else to allow your father to loot what rightly would belong to the Brazilian Government."

"Perhaps," Benjamin admitted. The suggestion did seem more likely than the fanciful idea of a mythical fountain offering youth to any who drank from it.

"What if there was another way?" Eliza said, which caught Benjamin off guard and he suspected the Home Secretary as well.

"Another way to what?" Benjamin asked.

"To beat them to the punch, to get to whatever the map leads to first."

"They spent two months outfitting a ship for this. Even if they were doing so circumspectly, I doubt we could do so much faster. We can't use the military, so we would have to approach 'The Treasury'." The last was said with a shudder by Sir Robert, who then continued, "By the time I acquired the funding and outfitted a ship, even if those loyal to THE Ministry didn't work against such efforts, and I'm sure they would, it would be months, and we would be far too far behind them in the chase."

"What you need then is a different kind of ship, Sir Robert, and I may be able to supply you with one for a price…" Eliza said with a mischievous edge to her voice.

"Miss Tu-Pa-Ka, I doubt there is a ship in the world that could make up a two-month lead, so unless you have one ready to sail tomorrow, I suspect whatever you're suggesting will be of little use," Sir Robert said.

"Oh, I think you will be surprised. Though it'll take a few weeks to build it, but I'm sure I can do so. He only ever drew the designs and built the engines and other components. I suspect right up until he died he was hoping your father would return and put the money in to complete it, Mr West. Perhaps you could do so in his stead," Eliza said.

"I'm sorry to say I don't follow you, Miss Tu-Pa-Ka," Sir Robert said, perplexed.

"You're not the only one," Benjamin agreed.

Eliza smiled at both of them, a charming and knowing smile that Benjamin found difficult to deal with. Nothing in his public-school education had ever equipped him to deal with a woman like Eliza Tu-Pa-Ka when she chose to smile that way.

"You will, I promise. Now Benjamin do you remember what your father wrote in his letter?"

"Yes, but I hardly see how that is relevant," he replied.

"What was his last instruction to you, Mr West?"

"What?" Benjamin asked, slightly agog and starting to blush profusely.

"The last thing in his letter?"

"You can't be serious?" he said, mildly horrified at the thought of repeating those words in front of Sir Robert.

"I assure you I am," she said, smiling that smile again.

"It said, I should ride… Are you serious, Eliza? You want me to restate that?"

"Word for word…"

"That I should ride Maybe's Daughter as he would have done…" Benjamin said and went a shade of purple that Eliza found delightfully amusing.

"I never explained what he was talking about, did I?" she said coyly.

"As I remember, you laughed at me, rather loudly," he replied with a mental shudder at the memory.

"Yes, I should apologise for that, but it really was quite amusing, because you see he said Maybe's Daughter. Not Tu-Pa-Ka's daughter. Maybe's Daughter…" she said as if that explained anything.

"Madam, I fail to see what strange messages Mr West's father sent him have to do with anything. Frankly the whole thing sounds quite indecent," Sir Robert interrupted.

Eliza smiled once more and failed to stifle a laugh at the expense of the two men in the room, or Benjamin suspected their whole gender. Then she explained.

"Yes, I can see how it might, but as I was pointing out just now, I'm not Maybe's Daughter, Sir Robert. I am MaeYaBee Tu-Pa-Ka's daughter. Maybe's Daughter, on the other hand, is what my father intended to name his airship…"

Chapter Seventeen

A Grand Enterprise

An airship… A ship designed to sail through the sky…

The idea was… Well, frankly the idea was absurd.

Except it wasn't.

At least in theory. Benjamin had, despite his own reservations, pointed this out to Sir Robert. The concept had been muted more than once in reputable scientific journals over the last thirty years or more, and Benjamin had found the idea thrilling as a boy, so had read many of the more fanciful papers. The dream of sailing around the sky went right back to when the Montgolfier brothers started making hot air balloons just after the turn of the century. The concept of powered flight had always been muted as feasible in the right circumstances, but the methods people had dreamed up over the years were almost always impractical. He had seen designs for huge wing-like oars that were meant to paddle through the sky. Out rigged sails attached to the sides of a balloon, generally drawn by men who had never gone aloft in such a contraption. With the age of steam, designs of giant screws to push air, like steam ships were pushed by propellers through the ocean ,were muted, but weight was always the problem, and many had deemed it as falling beyond the most basic laws of physics to solve the issue. Airships were a fool's dream consigned to fictions of the absurd.

Yet there, in Sir Robert's office, Eliza had told both him and the Home Secretary that not only had her father designed an airship, but he had built various test models for his design. Furthermore, he had designed and built special lightweight steam engines, improved by his condensers and the other workings. He had in fact solved all those insolvable problems and overcome the issue of weight. Aluminium, a metal considered rare and difficult to extract only a few decades before, was now cheap and plentiful in comparison, and Maybe had found ways to incorporate it in his designs, replacing steel and iron with it in his engines wherever he could. The project had been his passion right up until his death. His progress had been hampered only by lacking the funds to turn his models into a full-scale airship.

Eliza had explained all this to them and beaten back their collective scepticism. Then she went on to explain to them that most of his equipment was either in her father's workshop or in a small warehouse he owned a quarter mile away from his place of business. Indeed, he had progressed to the point that all that was really required was the construction of the air frame, helium and installation of the engines and other mechanical devices he had already constructed.

At one point in the discussion Sir Robert claimed, somewhat loftily, that for one man to solve all the problems that begat airship design stretched credulity. But Benjamin had pointed out that Stevenson had been solely responsible for The Rocket and solved many similarly considered insurmountable problems to build his first railways. When Sir Robert had scoffed at this comparison, Benjamin came to suspect Peel of a degree of that ugly British prejudice against those native to their colonies. Such men as Maybe had clearly been. The politician would deny any such prejudice on his part, Benjamin was sure, but it did not surprise him that even a man as educated as Sir Robert would harbour such common but ill-founded opinions. It did however disappoint him that this seemed to be the case.

He suspected Eliza, who had hidden it well if she noticed, would be even less enamoured of such opinions than he.

He tried not to dwell on this observation of the Home Secretary's character. By then he was somewhat caught up in the romance of it all. He had pointed out science was often advanced by lone individuals of talent and vision, which caused Sir Robert to raise an eyebrow of objection. But then Eliza had let slip that her father had made a habit of 'borrowing' the designs of other engineers. Anything in fact that might aid him in his project. Sir Robert seemed suitably mollified by this suggestion. Doubtless, Benjamin assumed, the minister had taken this to mean the greater part of the design was based on the solid work of British engineers. Thus they, rather than Maybe Tu-Pa-Ka, had been the real geniuses behind these new devices, and by extension the design of the airship as a whole.

A flicker of malicious amusement in Eliza's face caught Benjamin's eye at this point, and he suspected she had been entirely deliberate in her 'slip' about her father's 'borrowing of designs'. Just as he suspected that borrowing designs that 'slightly improved a rack and pinion' or for 'a new gauge that measured oil pressure with a little more accuracy' in no way detracted from the wider achievement of Maybe's design. But if Eliza was happy to play Sir Robert's prejudices off against him then Benjamin was not going to stand in her way.

'Given the money,' she had told them, 'to pay for its construction I could supervise it being built in a matter of weeks, two months at the most.' The cogitations of this she hardly needed to point out to them. With an airship they could set chase to Farnsworth, Wells and the rest. Air travel would doubtless prove far quicker, if Eliza's confidence was to be believed, than travelling by ship. Even if it could not match an ocean-bound ship for speed, an airship could fly a more direct route through the Amazon basin, unfettered as it would be by the need to follow the rivers and waterways.

And of course, as they had the only complete copy of the original map, they could not only catch up to THE Ministry's expedition but out strip them and beat them to the punch. Beat them and gain whatever it was the map finally led to. The map, Benjamin had cautioned himself, which Eliza had still not actually shown anyone. Nor would she, she informed them with a degree of indignation when they asked her to do so, because the map was her bargaining chip.

She would build them the ship alright; she was more than happy to see her father's dream come to fruition, but only if her terms were met. Of that Eliza was very determined, which in truth Benjamin was starting to think was her default state. Determined in the way the wind is determined to blow, or the tides determined to rise and fall. She was very much likened to a force of nature in that respect and damn him if he did not admire that about her. She was, frankly, unlike anyone he had ever met before, man or woman. Absurd though the idea of an airship might have sounded, when she said she could make it happen, he found himself wanting to believe her. If anyone could build such a thing, he decided, it was Eliza Tu-Pa-Ka.

Building it though was one thing, but her terms for doing so were something else. If she did undertake to do so then, she insisted, she would be aboard for its maiden voyage as chief engineer. She also informed the gentlemen that she would retain a third share in all patents generated by the construction of the damnable thing. The other shares would be held jointly by the West family and a government trust, so long as the Home Office put up half the cost of construction.

Yes, whole idea was absurd, as he kept telling himself. It was barking mad in fact...

And yet...

And yet somehow, with her winning smiles, boundless determination, and leaning heavily on all of this being a matter of the national interest, she had managed over the course of an hour to convince both Sir Robert and Benjamin himself to go along with the mad scheme. Indeed, they had agreed to jointly fund the building and outfitting of both her father's airship and the expedition to give chase to THE Ministry all the way to South America.

By the end of the discussions in the Home Secretary's office it had all made sense somehow.

Now though, as Gothe drove the carriage down to Cheapside, Benjamin sat half listening to Eliza still waxing lyrical about airship designs, buoyancy bladders, air sacks, helium, rotor turbines, small convection steam engines and a whole bunch of other things he barely understood at best, and he was starting to have second thoughts.

He was also, in fairness, having third thoughts. Thoughts of Benjamin West famous aeronaut. Captain of Great Britain's, indeed the world's, first true airship. Benjamin Edward West, the great pioneer of a new frontier.

B.E. West, Britannia's heroic master of the air...

It had a ring to it, he had to admit.

Only half listening to his companion, he sat back and considered what it all might mean. Not just the fame it could bring, or the renown. Not only that he would be sure to be invited to all the best parties. But also, that he would be investing in an enterprise that could change the nation as much as the railways had done only a decade or two before. Not just the nation, the empire, the whole damn world... Fortunes were to be made by being in on the ground floor of such ventures. The West family were already rich, it was true, but it was old money, and old money had been making way for new money of late. His grandfather, the family's patriarch, often bemoaned to Benjamin that he had to rub shoulders with railway barons and mill owners. 'Men of trade,' as he described them, 'They are taking over the country, my lad, and barely a real gentleman among them…'

Benjamin's grandfather was a man of definite opinions, and Benjamin found himself wondering what the old man would have to say about it all. That was going to be a conversation Benjamin was not entirely looking forward to. But with luck, it might be avoided. He had funds of his own to call upon first, and if it came to that, well, old money or not, his grandfather was a man who could see the potential in a venture such as this, he was sure.

"Whoa there…" he heard Gothe say to the horses from his perch in the driver's seat outside the carriage and they drew to a halt in a gloomy street. A glance through the window told Benjamin they had arrived at Maybe's Manufactory and done so just as dusk was setting in. The first whispers of the ever-prevalent river mist were already starting to roll in as the temperature dropped.

He stood and unlatched the door, before stepping out into the street and offering his hand to Eliza to help her down from the carriage, a sense of the unreality of it all still clouding his thoughts.

"That took a while," he shouted up to Gothe, who merely shrugged a reply, keeping hold of the reins in order to keep the horses in check. The beasts got skittish at this time of day.

"A steam wagon had broken down and was blocking Haymarket. I had to go the long way around," Gothe explained in his usual bland neutral tone.

Eliza took Benjamin's hand and climbed down, then stood for a moment adjusting her dress. She had worn her Sunday best for the meeting at Whitehall and had clearly not been entirely comfortable in the bustled dress. Women's fashions, as ever, were not well designed for sitting in carriages, so the whole ensemble needed to be pulled back into shape.

"I'll go gather my father's drawings then we can go down the warehouse and inspect the engines and what have you!" she told him briskly once she was done sorting out her dress.

"I'll come and help you," he said, offering mostly out of a desire to get in out of the cold as any wish to be helpful if he was honest about it. The breeze coming off the river held a chill that permeated his day attire.

"No need, I'll only be five minutes. I shall be quicker without your incessant questions anyway," she said and marched off in the direction of the main door to the shop.

"What questions?" he muttered to himself but let the comment slide as he watched her go. Instead he took a moment to enjoy the view. Which he enjoyed a little more than perhaps he should, he chided himself. There was, however, something about the way her bustle moved from side to side as she walked that he found hard not to admire.

As Eliza opened the unlocked door and disappeared into the workshop, he marvelled once again at just how forceful she could be. It was her sheer force of personality that had moved both him and the Home Secretary to agree to the plan. If anyone else had started suggesting to them that they finance the construction of an airship to chase off after rogue elements of the government, they would doubtless have been met with nothing but blank stares. But once Eliza got an idea in her head, she had a way of dragging you along with her. Damn him if he did not find her attractive when she did so. He could not help but admire her tenacity.

"That, Gothe, is a very strange woman," Benjamin said, though he was talking to himself as much as anything. He knew too well Gothe's opinions were things the former manservant seldom shared in any detail, so he wasn't seeking confirmation as such.

"Indeed, Sir…"

"Secretive too. I bet she has that map of hers in there somewhere and that's why she wants us waiting outside," Benjamin mused as it occurred to him.

"I couldn't say, Sir…"

"Yes, that's probably it, though you think if she was keeping it here, she would have had the good sense to keep the workshop locked, wouldn't you? And what's with this 'Sir' business, Gothe. You've never called me 'Sir' before."

"When one is treated like a servant, it behoves one to act as such… Sir," the hulking man chided.

"Oh, really, Gothe, when have I ever treated you like a…?"

"A moment… Did you say the workshop wasn't locked, West?" Gothe asked him, interrupting Benjamin's chain of thought.

"Well no, Miss Tu-Pa-Ka just walked in. I didn't see her use a key or anything, so it can't have been," West explained, puzzled by the expression on the former manservant's face. Gothe was hardly the most expressive of men, but Benjamin could tell when the man was puzzled by something. Just as he could tell when puzzlement shifted into worry. That, and the way Gothe was climbing down from the driver's seat and reaching for something out of the lock box that formed the foot plate, sent a shiver down the back of his neck that had nothing to do with the river breeze.

"What is it, Gothe…?" he started asking, then as he saw just what it was that Gothe was taking out of the footbox, worry turned to alarm. "Isn't that Maybe's gun?" he asked, which was akin to stating the obvious as there was no mistaking the six-cylinder shotgun revolver Gothe had last carried in anger at Sheers Wharf.

"The last time Miss Tu-Pa-Ka and I were here was when we were just setting off to save your skin, West," Gothe explained.

Benjamin felt a chill once more. The events at Sheers Wharf were something he would sooner forget all about in truth. "And?"

"And West, I locked that door. I remember doing so because the lock was new, what with the police breaking the previous one and all, and it was just a little too stiff for Miss Eliza to manage herself..." Gothe said.

The big man was already pushing past Benjamin, gun in hand, making for the entrance way with the slow steady walk of a man fully prepared to use the gun he carried.

Benjamin took a moment to grasp what his former manservant had explained, then as light dawned, he reached inside his coat for the revolver he did not have. He muttered, "Oh... Hell's teeth..." to himself for the mistake of leaving the gun in his desk at home, then, in a manner not befitting a gentleman, he set off after Gothe, overtaking the big man just before he got to the doorway and dived through it himself.

"Eliza, Harrington's here!" he shouted as loudly as he could as he pitched into the darkness of the workshop.

"I know!" came an even-tempered reply from up in the office, a reply Benjamin just had time to hear before the long piece of two by four, a blunt weapon if ever there was one, wielded by Mr Instrument, made contact with his head and sent him reeling backwards into darkness...

Chapter Eighteen

Whence it Came to Pass

"I know," Eliza called out coldly, keeping her eyes on the revolver pointed in her direction, the revolver in the hands of her enemy.

Harrington was propping himself up against her father's desk, ten feet away. Eliza noted with some minor pride that his left leg was strapped and bound to hold it stiff and there was dried blood around a long tear in his trousers, doubtless due to the bullet wound she had inflicted, and a backstreet surgeon's efforts to remove the bullet. With any luck the wound would turn nasty and get infected. Despite the leering grin he was giving her, she could tell he was in pain. Not enough for her liking but in pain all the same. That alone was some compensation for the position she now found herself in.

"Ah, do we have a brave knight in shining armour rushing to save the damsel? How very fairy-tale this all is," he said, the spiteful sarcasm clear in his voice. "The gentleman you've so wrapped around your finger, is it?"

"I've no one wrapped round my finger," she snapped back at him and made to raise her right hand and let her derringer slip free... The derringer which wasn't there. Going into Whitehall armed was 'not the done thing' as West had told her. She cursed him silently as she remembered, her arm already halfway up. She stopped regardless, as Harrington pulled back the hammer on the revolver, cocking it, so that the merest touch on the trigger would fire it.

"Oh no, arms by your side, Miss Maybe, you can keep your nasty little peashooters out of harm's way." He told her, and she did as he bid, much as it pained her.

At least if he assumes I'm armed that may help, she thought to herself. It was a scant consolation for not having her derringers with her, but it was all the advantage she had. She could rush him of course, but chances were he would fire before she crossed the distance between them, and if he did... Well, he could hardly miss.

There was a great clattering from the workshop below. It sounded like someone had just fallen heavily into some of the boxes stacked by the doorway. West, she assumed. She did not doubt for a moment that Harrington had at least one of his pet thugs down there, if not more. West, she knew all too well, would charge through the doors without thinking. *Damn fool*, she thought, then chided herself. *Says me. The door wasn't locked. I should've known something was up when the door wasn't locked.* She kicked herself for being too busy revelling in her victories at the Home Office to take note of the obvious.

She shook herself, physically and mentally, then met her enemy's stare with her own.

"What do you want, Harrington?" she half snarled at him.

He sneered back in return and gave her a nasty smile.

"Want? I want nothing, my dear Miss Maybe. Thanks in no small part to you, my card has been marked. I'm a wanted man, don't you know? And all because you wouldn't see reason and sell those damn papers to me when I offered a fair price. You and your damn father," he said, and in his eyes she could see a tinge of desperation.

"Leave my father out of this," she said as calmly as she could.

"Would that I could, darling, would that I could. You know he'd be right proud of you, I'm sure. You're as stubborn as he was. Damn darkie bastard, always swanning around like he's a damn native. Thinking he is too good for the likes of us that were born here. Yet I treated him fair, so I did, fairer than he deserved, and what thanks did I get?"

There was another loud crash downstairs. It seemed that West was not quite done yet. Harrington did not seem to notice; he was too busy venting his spleen.

"Couldn't just take the money could he. Had to stand on principle," he said and spat on the office floor. In his moment of distraction, she almost made a move, but he was too fast for her, snapping his gaze back and making a point of sighting down the barrel of his gun. "Now, now, take a step back there, Miss. I've not finished talking, so I haven't. It would be a shame to shoot you too soon."

She did as he bid, watching the shaking hand that held the revolver. It struck her it was apt to go off at any time, whether he meant to shoot or no, such was the tremble in his hand. More evidence of the pain he must be in from the leg wound.

"Fine," she said. "The further away from your stinking breath I stand the better." She was unable to stop herself antagonising the swine. Though she was grateful for another reason. The step back had taken her closer to the doorway, and to where her father kept a billy club in an old umbrella stand, which was now temptingly close to hand. But only if she could get him to come to close enough to her that she could use it.

He laughed, that same horrible laugh of his that made her skin crawl. "Oh, my breath stinks, does it? I'm sure it does, dear. Now you hang around with gentlemen, but they will tire of you soon enough, you and your dark skin. A man like that may plough the odd dark furrow but he weds good English pasture, you mark my words."

"I don't know what you're implying," Eliza said, inching backwards a little more, trying to buy herself time.

"Oh, I'm sure you do, Miss Maybe, I'm sure you do. You darkies are all the same, flaming heathens, you all rut like the beasts you are," he said, still leering at her, half excited by his own vulgarity she was sure.

Least ways, she thought with a certain spitefulness, *if he's a man still capable of getting excited in such a way.*

Eliza returned his venomous glare. She wasn't surprised by his words, there were plenty in Cheapside and beyond who harboured such opinions. Even among those who were outwardly friendly towards her and her father. 'He was a fine man for a darkie…' more than one had probably thought at his funeral. Not that they would say such a thing of course, at least not when they thought she was in earshot. But she had heard such words muttered behind his back and her own, more times than she cared to count. Sometimes it was just ignorance talking, oh it hurt, but it was nothing more than that, no real spite behind it, just fools talking. People too stupid to know how stupid they were. Other times though, words like that were said with venom, and real hatred. She found it ironic that they accused the dark skinned of being no better than beasts while they spoke and acted out of base tribalism themselves. It was always easy to hate the other, the Jew, the dark skinned, the foreigner. It was easy to hate, and easy to blame the other for your own inadequacies.

All too damn easy…

That Harrington was a man who harboured such opinions did not surprise her in the slightest. It was, ironically, just one more reason to hate him. She suspected now he was working himself up to killing her, giving himself more reasons to do so by venting his hatreds. Harrington had never been one to do his own dirty work. She suspected he had never pulled the trigger or wielded the blade himself before now. Men like him seldom did, they had others to do that for them, all the while keeping their own hands clean.

She noticed something else as well. Harrington had always put on airs and graces before. He had always talked like he was an educated man. Oh, his utterances were rough around the edges, sure, but it was enough to fool the locals in Cheapside that he had some form of breeding to him. Yet here and now, when he had been driven into a corner by Inspector Grace and his runners, his words and accent were more reminiscent of the street scum, he surely was.

He's nervous, well good, let him be nervous, nervous people make mistakes, she thought to herself, still edging towards the umbrella stand. Though she could not rid herself of another thought. *Nervous people also strike out before they're ready...* He could shoot her at any point she realised all too well.

There was the sound of heavy boots on the stairs.

Heavy lumbering boots...

"Ah, now that will be Mr Instrument. He has a bone to pick with you as well. He was surprisingly fond of Mr Blunt, quite an item they were, came up together. You know I've half a mind to let him have some fun with you before I finish you off. And trust me, girl, when he is through with you, you'll be begging me to put you out of your misery. Oh yes... But before I do, I want what's due to me. I'm out in the cold thanks to you and your gentleman friend. My employers cut ties with me after the wharf, did you know that? Bunch of posh bastards didn't like it when things got too dirty for them. I should've known better, weak stomachs their kind. Now coppers I've been paying off for years would soon as do me in as catch me, and Cheapside is too damn hot for old Harrington, yes, it is."

"About time they ran you off, swine," she told him, now inches away from being able to grab the billy club, much good it would do her. She had scant chance with it against even an enfeebled Harrington while he held a revolver. She would have no chance against Mr Instrument. The club would probably bounce off him, the gorilla that he was. But she was desperate, and it was the only chance she had. *Just a little more*, she thought, trying to encourage herself as a shadow loomed through the frosted glass of the office window.

"The word is you were holding out on me. The noobs think the map you gave up was missing a bit, so they sent word down to Cheapside that if I could get it from you then they'd see me right after all. But the thing is, Miss Maybe, I've been stashing money away for years. So, I'm half inclined to say 'sod yea' to the lot of them. I'll just kill you now and they will be stuck without their damn map and I'll get myself a ship to America, so I will. It's the great land of opportunity they say, and I've always been a man to take his opportunities. But I'll tell you what, I'm a fair man, so I is, so I will give you one chance and one chance only. Give over the real map now and I'll make it quick... I can't say fairer than that. Can I now...?"

She laughed, not out of misplaced bravado. She was not 'laughing in the face of fear'. She laughed because it was all too absurd. What kind of threat was 'I'll kill you quick rather than slow'? Dead was dead either way. And she laughed because it put him on edge, and maybe, just maybe that would be enough.

So, she laughed and then made her move, grabbing for the billy club, just as the door came crashing open as Mr Instrument, she assumed, made his grand entrance.

"What the..." Harrington shouted out, and the gun went off.

Eliza was struck by a bolt of pure white pain as the bullet hit her, and right then, she knew she was dead...

Chapter Nineteen

Dead Once More

She was not quite dead yet.

The bullet went through her shoulder. Harrington had shot high and right, not quite but almost missing his original target. Half because she was diving for the club, and half because he was not really shooting at her at all.

She spun through the air and came crashing down against the wall, by chance, the impact of the bullet throwing her out of the way.

Harrington's pistol went off again, but as he shot there was a second louder rumble. Like a burst of thunder striking inside the room itself.

The shock of being shot blinded her for a moment, but as her vision cleared she found herself looking up at Gothe, standing in the doorway, her father's shotgun in his hands, still smoking from the two top barrels.

The pain of the bullet wound was making her shake. She was unable to think straight, but she managed to push herself up against the wall so she could turn her gaze in the direction of Harrington. There wasn't much left of him to see. At close quarters Gothe had taken the man's head clean from his shoulders. Blood and brains were splattered on the wall behind the body. Despite the pain, she found herself laughing once more, laughing, shaking and unable to keep her eyes focused.

"Eliza, Gothe..." she heard someone shouting from the workshop below. Then she could hear running on the stairs. West, she assumed, West was coming. What had Harrington called him? Her knight in shining armour. *Some damn knight,* she thought bitterly to herself, *arriving after the battle's done*, and then she tried to laugh some more. But the sound she made seemed wrong, weak somehow.

Distant, as if it was coming from someone else.

She looked over at Gothe just as her hulking protector turned to face her. Then her eyes widened as she saw his face. The right side of it just was not there, the black oozing stuff he had instead of blood was sliding down a ruined cheek. His right eye was gone, as was a portion of his skull. As his remaining eye met hers, she saw the slightest of smiles cross his blood-soaked lips and what could have been the slightest of nods of recognition towards her. Then the big man tumbled to the floor like a tree as it was felled by a lumberjack.

"Oh god, Gothe!" she heard a voice saying, and hardly recognised it as her own.

Then a moment later West appeared where Gothe had stood. Entering the room, he seemed to be trying to take everything in at once. The headless body of Harrington. Her propped up against the wall, blood running from the wound just below her shoulder. Then finally he looked down at his former manservant, and looking at his face he must have wondered, as she was now, if Gothe was lying there dead, instead of just sort of alive. That look suggested the worst, suggested what she was sure of herself. No one could have survived that much damage, no matter what weird stuff pumped through their veins.

The principles of triage must have kicked in, for West now ignored Gothe completely and rushed over to her. His face was utterly ashen, his grip on himself tenuous at best. She wondered in a cloudy, absent way just how much West was desperate for a drink right then. But it appeared when needs must he could forgo getting half-drunk before needing to attend to surgery…

Her mind wandered for a moment, and she tried to remember just how long it had been since the two of them had operated on Gothe downstairs in this very workshop. The day of her father's funeral. A day she could not help but remember. Yet she couldn't remember how long ago that had been. Days, just a few days, she was sure. Why couldn't she remember…? Why couldn't she…?

"Put your hand here," West said sharply, his voice dragging her back to the present. He took hold of her left hand and forced her to put it over the hole in her shoulder, but not before shoving a handkerchief of all things into it to help stem the bleeding.

She did as she was told. For once it seemed the right thing to do, but she felt weak, and she started slipping from full consciousness again. Her eyelids felt heavy and she was finding it hard to keep her head up. Her hand felt wet, and oddly warm. What was that beneath her fingers…?

Her cheek stung following the slap that hit her unawares and jarred her back into consciousness.

"Stay awake, damn you. I'll not lose two friends today," West half screamed at her, forcing her hand firmer against her wound. "Keep the damn pressure on. Push harder," he seemed to be saying, it was hard to distinguish his words.

She did what she could, her mind whirling. *Not lose two friends… what did he mean not lose two friends…?* she found herself wondering as she heard a clattering of things hitting the floor. He was shoving everything off one of her father's drawing boards. *What was the man doing, damn him. This is father's office, how dare he*, she thought and the world went a little grey once more. She wanted to berate him for making a mess. But she knew there was some reason she should not do so, though she could not think why right at that moment…

Then he was taking her in his arms and struggling to lift her. She tried to help, to not be such a dead weight. *Dead weight...* the thought came. *Dead, oh god, Gothe, he meant Gothe, oh god...* The memory from just a few moments earlier hit her. *How did I forget so soon, Gothe, poor Gothe.* She started to struggle in West's arms so she could turn and see if Gothe was moving. But now he had her up he was too strong for her or was it she was too damn weak in her condition to struggle against him.

He laid her on the drawing board, which he had levelled out to act as a table. Laying her on her chest, he moved her left hand back into place, covering the wound in her shoulder. Her head tilted now, she could see Gothe lying on the office floor. It didn't look like he was breathing. She sought desperately for signs of life in the former manservant but couldn't see any, even the slightest movement.

Not breathing but did he ever? she found herself thinking and something in her wanted to laugh at the thought. It was just one more absurd question in a day of absurdities. But the world was getting cloudy again and she was aware that West was doing something to the back of her dress.

For some reason she could not quite grasp at, she needed him to stop. He couldn't undo her dress. Not because it was improper. In fact, now she thought about it, she admitted to herself that she would not mind if it was because it was improper, no matter what Harrington had implied. But there was another reason, she knew there was another reason, but could not grasp at it. *Why can't I let him undo my dress?* she thought, panicking now.

"Please Eliza, calm down. I need to stem the bleeding. The bullet went clean through, so that's good, less chance of infection. But I need to get at the wound to stem the bleeding." He was telling her, and she could feel him pulling at the strings that held the back of her dress together. Pulling them loose, undoing them.

"No, stop, you can't," she said weakly, and found herself panicking once more, desperately trying to remember why she couldn't let him do so.

"Eliza, calm down, please. I've got to do this. Don't worry, it's not like I haven't seen a woman's back before," he was saying as he pulled the last tie free and she felt him pull the dress apart, down and around her shoulders.

And then he stopped.

He actually stopped.

And for a moment she held her breath. Hoping he had not gone too far. Then he said…

"Oh… Oh I see," and he suddenly let out a strange little laugh. "Oh my…"

It was then Eliza remembered what it was she did not want him to find.

"So that's where you hid the map. Oh my, you really are a clever girl, Miss Tu-Pa-Ka, and a clever girl who is going to live, thankfully. I think so at any rate, so a lucky girl as well as a clever one," he told her, the laughter still in his voice, as he set about stemming the bleeding which appeared to him to be centred around the compass icon on the top right hand corner of the map. The bullet had passed through right at the point where all directions met.

Eliza, on the verge of passing out, her left-hand still clamped over the entry wound, swung her right arm as well as she could to slap out at West, finding a reserve of strength as yet untapped to do the one thing she could and berate him…

"As I told Sir Robert, it's woman, Mr West. Clever WOMAN."

Epilogue

"So, they are going ahead with their plan to build an airship?" the first of the two men said, nursing a rather good single malt as he relaxed in the highbacked leather chair. The Spartacus Club always had the best single malts. He was pleased, for this reason alone, that he had chosen it as the location for this meeting.

"Yes, I must say I'm surprised you are allowing them to do so, they're set against you after all," the other man replied.

"Indeed. Well, as it is said, one must keep one's enemies close… They also have the only complete map, as you know. I must compliment you, you did well setting them on this course. They don't suspect your real loyalties, I take it?"

"Why would they? Though I'm sure it would be a damn sight less tiresome to arrest the woman and simply force her to supply us with the location of her map."

"Not so, besides the surgeon, our Mr West engaged to tend to Miss Tu-Pa-Ka's wounds was most illuminating on that score," the first man said, with a smile that on anyone else the other man would have considered mischievous.

"She told the surgeon. You mean you know where it is?" he asked, surprised.

"She didn't tell him so much as show him, and while he was technically sworn to secrecy by Mr West, he is a member of another club I frequent from time to time, and loose of lip when he has a good scotch in him. Hippocratic oath or not."

"So then, where is it? Why have you not dispatched men to obtain it?" the other man asked, his moustache bristling with no little indignation.

"Because it is no longer of importance."

"No longer of importance, after the lengths we went to obtain it in the first place. A man died; several men died in fact. How can you say it's of no importance now, Mr Wells?"

The first man scowled at the use of his name. Even though they were in the Spartacus, there were forms to uphold. He was after all not supposed to be in the country anymore, and there was a value in anonymity.

"Because it is not. This airship they plan to build makes it so. Airships are the future, and this will be the first of many to be built on the back of MaeYaBee Tu-Pa-Ka's designs. Years before the Zeppelin brothers are even out of nappies. It will alter history, this first airship and its maiden voyage. Benjamin West may even become a national hero, if things play out right. Doubtless it will be a shame that the first airship captain and his engineer will never return with their ship. But he deserves any credit that comes his way, don't you think? As for Miss Tu-Pa-Ka, well she will most likely be conveniently forgotten by history. A footnote at best. History is seldom kind to women, no matter how deserving. But the ship… The ship will be remembered and replicated for the empire's use."

"But if they have the map, then they will beat your man to the fountain. Doesn't that scupper your plans somewhat, Wells?"

"Oh, my dear Sir, you really should be more careful using my name like that. I've plans for you. The new greater Britannia will need a new Prime Minister in time, so don't sour the deal we made by second guessing me now. And think, man, an airship needs a crew after all, not just a captain and an engineer, but a full crew. And who else will they turn to supply them with a crew but their auspicious partner in all this and with you picking out their crew, Sir Robert... Well, I'm sure the fountain will fall into our hands right on schedule. The Empire will never see the sun set upon it, and the Queen will reign in perpetuity, just as I've planned." H G Wells told the Home Secretary, and sat back into the folds of the armchair, drinking his scotch and smiling beneath his moustache.

The future was easy to plan when you're its master after all.

THE END

ABOUT THE AUTHOR

Mark writes novels that often defy simple genre definitions, they could be described as speculative fiction, though Mark would never use the term as he prefers not to speculate.

When not writing novels Mark is a persistent pernicious procrastinator, he recently petitioned parliament for the removal of the sixteenth letter from the Latin alphabet.

He is also 7th Dan Blackbelt in the ancient Yorkshire martial art of EckEThump and favours a one man one vote system but has yet to supply the name of the man in question.

Mark has also been known to not take bio very seriously.

Email: Darrack@hotmail.com

Twitter: @darrackmark

Blog: https://markhayesblog.com/

Printed in Poland
by Amazon Fulfillment
Poland Sp. z o.o., Wrocław